Anna's
Secret Legacy

◆ ◆ ◆ ◆ ◆ ◆ ◆ ◆ ◆

By S.A. Williams

INFINITY
PUBLISHING

Copyright © 2009 by S.A. Williams aka Anna's Legacy
Copyright © 2010 by S.A. Williams
WGA

ISBN 0-7414-5828-4

Printed in the United States of America

Published September 2010

INFINITY PUBLISHING
1094 New DeHaven Street, Suite 100
West Conshohocken, PA 19428-2713
Toll-free (877) BUY BOOK
Local Phone (610) 941-9999
Fax (610) 941-9959
Info@buybooksontheweb.com
www.buybooksontheweb.com

Special thanks to Laura Brooks and Don Eichman for their constant
encouragement, time and editorial support.

Many thanks to Peter Allen for his knowledge of maps and trains. To M. Grady for
encouraging me to write this. Special thanks to Bill Ewing, Gerry Lenfest, Lynn
Hendee, Tom Boehning,Don Eichman, Tom Haas, Charlie Kendall, Micki Williams,
Dick Fox, Steve Harmelin, Carole Gravagno, Bernie Resnick, Bill Avery, Catlin
Adams, Melanie Mayron, Yaniv Aronson, Heather McCarthy, Dorine Kunst, Grace
Lowe Russak,Catherine Evich, Ray Carballada, Andy Williams, Mark Forker, and all
the guys at Shooters Post Production for believing in my project and to my many
friends who spent countless hours listening to me talk about this project. Thank you.

Thanks to The Library of Congress and The Free Library of Philadelphia.

This book is dedicated to my Dad, Jennifer and Christopher—I love you!

Prologue

PARIS
SPRING 1940

Anna was dying. She felt as if she were watching everything from a distance with calm detachment. She knew she should be terrified and desperate. But all of that seemed beyond her. Anna sensed herself lifting, moving up and out of her body as if she were floating in warm water. She felt herself roll and tumble, and turned to see her body sprawled amid the debris of her sitting room. Blood was everywhere.

The couch cushions had been slashed, their puffy guts yanked out. Both end tables were on their sides. One lamp had shattered; the other lay intact on the ground, its shade knocked away, the yellow light spilling out over the millions of tiny shards of glass that surrounded her body. It was as if she were floating in space surrounded by twinkling stars, adrift forever. In the invisible current, Anna saw herself dying among the glass splinters.

Memory was fragmented. She tried to grasp the how and why of her sprawled body and the blood seeping from the gash on her head. A shadowy vision of two handsome American men clicked into place, and some vague disturbing event from earlier that day. The ruble still hung from the fine gold chain under her sweater. Then everything went black.

It had all started seven weeks ago.

♦ ♦ ♦ ♦ ♦ ♦ ♦ ♦ ♦

1

The Research Lab—Copenhagen, Denmark
April 1940

DAYS BEFORE THE GERMAN INVASION
OF NORWAY AND DENMARK

In silence, a solitary figure quickly pushed the door open to a white-walled research lab. A slim, intense blonde woman with a determined expression on her face walked to her microscope.

It must work this time, she thought. *After three years of nonstop research, I know the answer is in here, in this bit of solution.*

The solution itself was an anomaly: it represented several years' worth of research derived from water taken from a Russian hot sulphur spring long ago. Anna quickly pushed a loose blonde strand back into her ponytail and pulled her stool closer to the microscope, muttering,

"There *must* be a blueprint that our cells recognize from this sulphur water which helps them reset to their original healthy molecular structure."

After a few moments, she abruptly pushed back her stool in frustration and stood. Still for a moment, she again considered the microscope in front of her. Sighing, she began to pace the floor, her hands stuffed in her pockets and her brow furrowed.

Her eyes, a light violet blue, were reminiscent of the same color streak particularly visible in the sky before a spectacular sunset. In the left pocket of her white lab coat, she rubbed together two gold rubles that she always kept with her, a nervous habit she had begun as a young teenager in Russia.

♦   ♦   ♦   ♦   ♦   ♦   ♦   ♦   ♦   ♦

Waiting at the end of the dark street below, two men hide in the murky shadows. One man glanced at his watch impatiently. Taking a strong drag on his filterless cigarette, he flicked it to the ground, simultaneously exhaling and stomping it out with a smash of his boot. They both looked up towards the light still on in the second-floor lab.

Lukas and his partner Finn had been specifically deployed to recruit any resources to aid the Führer in his quest for scientific knowledge. Since Hitler had come into power in 1933, science, medicine and technology had become of utmost importance, and he had called for a spirit of "Gleichschaltung" (marching in step). The Kaiser Wilhelm Institute was producing poison gas and numerous other experiments.

Hitler's need for increasing the scope of applied science and technology for war-making assumed a new urgency. A special group of assassins, trained and skilled in the ways of brutal persuasion, would help expedite this process. Lukas and Finn, who excelled in their training, were proud to be a part of this group. They were assigned to recruit, kill and gather resources, especially scientists, in Copenhagen.

♦   ♦   ♦   ♦   ♦   ♦   ♦   ♦   ♦

Back in the lab, Anna thought out loud again,

"The sulphur water comes from deep in the earth; therefore, it must contain a molecular sequencing capable of surviving in a hostile environment and regenerating over millions of years. Just like a starfish with its five points." She puzzled through her train of thought.

I know somehow this all makes sense. If I can figure out what secret this water contains, I can determine what properties are unique and recreate it. Ingested, it could contain repair functions that could cure aged or diseased cells or, at the very least, protect the cell membrane, making it invincible to disease. There are only twenty known amino acids, and all proteins of life are made by a combination of these twenty. I know the answer is here if I can figure out the mathematical sequencing.

She strode back to her lab station again and looked hard at the vial which contained the sulphur water. She had brought it with her from Russia and had kept it sealed, airtight, for many years until she started to work on her doctoral degree. The subject of her thesis was on protein structure and the vast combinations of amino acids.

Now a respected research scientist in her early thirties, Anna had been working for three years at The Niels Bohr Institute in Copenhagen after having completed her doctorate in biology at Oxford University.

She had gravitated to research in her quest to unlock the mystery of the sulphur water as a possible way to help her younger sister, Britta, who had hemophilia. Her motivation to find a cure for Britta's condition sparked her interest in Ayurveda, the 5,000-year-old system of natural healing which had its origins in the Vedic culture of India, as well as traditional Chinese medicine and Tibetan medicine.

Shortly after she completed her Oxford research studies, Dr. Spelman had recruited her to research the composition of this water at The Niels Bohr Institute here in Copenhagen. They had been working meticulously for the past few years, determined to unlock the liquid's secrets, and guided by Anna's theory of the restorative properties of sulphur water, trying to find a way to recreate the molecular structure so that they could reproduce a restorative draught.

The premise was straightforward—if, in fact, water from a hot sulphur spring—for reasons of heat, pressure and the chemical composition of the earth's crust in a particular locale—could produce bacteria that evolved in a manner completely different than any other life form, then this bacteria—having existed and lived in a hostile environment—could have evolved with sophisticated methods of self-repair.

They speculated that it was reasonable to think that when these bacteria die, their membranes would rupture and spill their protein into the surrounding water. Based on the study of protein structure linked together in different sequences, if the code could be unraveled, it might contain the answer to the repair of damaged cellular organelles. Imagine! This serum could be the cure-all for the ages. Millions of lives could be saved. Millions would be safe from disease and against what the experts were calling germ warfare

Her mentor at Oxford, Dr. Cunningham, had told her, "There are no fancy tricks; it's work, work, work and repetition, repetition, repetition—until you get it right."

Recalling this, Anna glanced quickly at the back wall lined with cages of test mice and rabbits. Some were ailing and some were healthy. The ones that had been injected with the sulphur water serum were all doing fine. However, there was very little serum left, and the need to be able to recreate this became increasingly urgent.

She moved back to the stool and sat down again, looking somewhat discouraged at the piles of folders and notes on her desk.

I'm going to keep going until I get it right.

Leaning forward, she breathed in deeply and held her breath. She reached for the medicine dropper next to her containing the special solution, and placed two drops onto the slide on the microscope's platform. Slowly, the liquids on the slide began to converge. She leaned back again and closed her eyes—a determined, hopeful expression visible. Almost immediately and to her utter amazement, the light bulb beside her face, which was attached to the underbelly of the slide, illuminated. As she exhaled, a smile slowly spread across her face.

2

The Niels Bohr Institute—Copenhagen
April 1940

This miraculous discovery was a medical breakthrough of enormous proportions. It was a formula that could change the world forever. Anna knew this discovery must be kept secret, no matter what the cost. If in fact, the formula could restore a damaged cell membrane, the possibility existed that it could be chemically manipulated to also destroy cell membranes. Ingested in the water supply, it could wipe out humanity. In the wrong hands, mass devastation would occur if the mathematical sequencing was discovered.

She furiously began to write out the details of her discovery in her research notebook, coding the bacteria-produced proteins as a sequence of alpha letters. Then she tore out the last page and stuffed it in her lab coat pocket. Glancing at the wall clock, she was surprised to see that it was already ten o'clock and pitch dark outside.

I must get this on microfilm and take it home with me for safekeeping, she thought, experiencing a strange euphoria mixed with anxiety. She stood up and realized her hands were shaking. She allowed herself a moment to recover while carefully putting away the remaining small amount of serum in a locked, vacuum-sealed container. Quickly she made her way to the adjacent microfilm room and copied the formula onto microfilm. She hid the small bit of film inside her brassiere.

Grabbing her coat and scarf, she flipped off the lights and, with keys jingling from her still shaking hands, locked the lab. The sound of her running footsteps filled the corridor as she headed toward the rear stairs. Unexpectedly, a lab door opened in front of her.

"Anna, what are you doing here so late?" exclaimed Dr. Charles de Hevesy, highly regarded as one of the most esteemed scientists at the Institute.

Startled, Anna stopped in her tracks.

"Dr. de Hevesy! Good evening," cursing inwardly as she had hoped to leave the lab as quickly as possible.

"Come, you must see my latest update on my 'Aqua Regia' progress," he cried heartily as he waved her into the room.

She turned and followed him in, not wanting to seem in too much of a hurry.

"Anna, remember our discussion about my process of 'Aqua Regia?' How I can remove gold from an object, place it in liquid suspension and then replace it on the object?"

His mischievous brown eyes took in one of his favorite young associates. He found Anna to be one of those mysterious creatures—a compelling mixture of intelligence, charm, innocence and beauty. He knew instinctively he could trust her.

"Here, take a look," he urged. "Do you remember my two friends, Max Laue and James Franck, who won Nobel Prize medals? Well, have a look at this!"

He pointed proudly to a large jar filled with yellow liquid sitting on his desk.

"They loaned me their medals, and I have removed the gold from them. Should those Nazi devils plan on coming here, well, they would think nothing of a plain jar with a yellow solution containing hydrochloric acid. In fact, I will label it 'Urine,' " he exclaimed, his eyes dancing with mirth.

"At a later date, I can replace the gold back onto their medals."

"Dr. de Hevesy, this is amazing!" cried Anna, who, in her first few weeks at the Institute, had recognized his genius. "Shall we have a try with my lucky rubles?" She laughed lightly although her eyes betrayed her seriousness.

He looked at her curiously with an astute question waiting to be asked. He let her continue.

"If the Nazis invade, I should hate for them to have my only mementos from my father," she explained quickly. She reached into her pocket, pulled out the two gold rubles and handed the coins to him.

"These are quite rare—are you sure?" asked Dr. de Hevesy, who slowly turned over the rubles, looking at the slightly askew image of Nicholas II stamped on the coins.

"They are Russian ten-ruble gold coins, a present from my father on my fifteenth birthday," commented Anna

"These coins are a fascinating relic of Imperial Russia under Nicholas II, the last Czar of Russia before the Bolshevik revolution, minted from 1897 to 1911," as he handed her back the rubles.

"Yes, that's right. On one side there is a slightly raised bust profile of the head of Czar Nicholas II that was slightly askew, and thus had been discarded as defective," Anna explained. "The coins were manufactured in the mint where my father worked when I was a child, and he brought these discarded ones home as a present for me. It is ironic that they are so valuable today."

Anna thought of Britta's hemophilia but said nothing. She wanted to share her discovery with him, instinctively knowing he would keep her secret. Not wanting to burden him, she decided to keep silent for the moment.

"I trust you to put the gold back on at another time. After all, wouldn't they help you to prove your theory?" asked Anna.

Dr. de Hevesy hesitated for a moment.

"My dear Anna, these are pure gold; I would suggest you keep them as they are—a wonderful tribute to another time in history, a loving gift from your father, as well as for good luck. If you change your mind, we can do it then. Please be careful. I fear the land of Goethe and Wagner is taking a turn for the worse. My colleagues are quite concerned that Copenhagen and other European cities will be the target of a German takeover. How much of this speculation is true remains to be seen, but my recommendation is to be very, very cautious. And, Anna," he added, looking at her intently, "do keep your research under lock and key."

Anna again considered telling him about her discovery and its implications for her sister Britta, but quickly decided that this was not the right time. In fact, she needed to hurry home. Lately, Britta had been so weak that she had needed to stay in bed from morning till night, and Anna was very concerned.

She smiled fondly at her Hungarian friend.

"Thank you, Dr. de Hevesy. I do believe you should get the Nobel Prize for this." She gave him a quick hug, then pounded down the stairs, flung open the rear door of the building and ran into the darkness of the night, darting down the narrow alleyway between two rows of buildings.

If only he knew how true his words are.

◆　◆　◆　◆　◆　◆　◆　◆　◆

At the end of the dark street, the same two men were still hiding impatiently in the shadows. Their steely eyes focused on the front door, watching and waiting for Anna with more than just passing curiosity. Where was she? She should have emerged by now. The Sicherheitsdienst, the secret and deadly sister agency to the better-known Gestapo, would reward them very highly for the capture of this female scientist, but more importantly, Dr. Spelman would surely hand over his research.

♦ ♦ ♦ ♦ ♦ ♦ ♦ ♦ ♦ ♦

Lukas and Finn were hidden in the shadows of the trees that were blowing in the bitingly cold night wind. Lukas exhaled and mashed his cigarette out with his boot. As he turned back to see the front door of the lab open and a man emerge, the streetlight revealed the outline of a swastika tattoo on the back of his neck.

"Is she with him?" he asked.

Finn shook his head.

The man closed and locked the front door of the Institute. He wrapped a scarf around his neck, oblivious to the world around him. The building was now dark and silent.

Lukas jabbed Finn hard in the ribs. "Damn, we missed her again," he growled as he spit on the ground.

♦ ♦ ♦ ♦ ♦ ♦ ♦ ♦ ♦ ♦

Reflecting on her discovery, Anna sprinted through the labyrinth of alleyways that crisscrossed between the houses and tenements, her breath coming in ragged bursts. She slipped on the icy pavement and threw out her hand against the building beside her to catch her balance. She quickly glanced over her shoulder and saw no one. The only footsteps echoing in the still of the night were her own.

With the microfilm tucked inside her bra along with the last page of her research notebook, Anna recalled that her fascination with the sulphur water started in childhood. *Home, what is that?* she thought. *There is no home. Our village was completely wiped out by the earthquake, along with the sulphur spring.*

She fiercely clenched her fists as she walked, ignoring the stinging wind. Though no one could possibly know what she carried, she saw each passing face as a foe. She finally arrived at the dimly lit doorstep of a brick townhouse and knocked gently as she pulled her keys from her coat pocket to open the door.

Britta might be sleeping, she thought, but the door opened immediately. Anna quickly entered the small townhouse, closed the door and locked it securely behind her.

"Britta," said Anna, hugging her sister, unable to contain herself, "I have finally figured out the formula for the mystery of the sulphur springs, the missing link in the equation, the master switch to make it work."

Anna continued in a rush of excitement.

"Tomorrow before dawn, we will go to the lab so I can give it to you. I know it will work. Trust me. Get some sleep now. We must get to the lab very early before anyone else arrives. If I am caught, I will surely lose my position at the Institute."

The dark circles blackening Britta's eyes made her look much older than her twenty years. She wrapped her bathrobe more tightly around her as she sat down on the couch and held her knees close to her chest,

"I don't like your grouchy boss anyway. I am scared, Anna. What if it doesn't work?" Britta's eyes filled with tears.

Anna touched her face gently.

"I promise it will be all right. Just think how it will be when you are well. Injecting you with the serum is the only way."

Britta looked up and nodded her head.

"All right, Anna. If there is no other choice, we might as well try it."

Anna spoke forcefully then.

"No one else can know what I have discovered. This formula in the wrong hands would put our world in great danger. You are the only person I trust."

Britta nodded again and painfully walked up the stairs to her bedroom, leaving Anna to sit alone in deep thought as she gazed at the dying embers in the fireplace.

The small window that faced the street gave the impression that it was bitter cold. It had started raining outside. Anna poked at the embers of the fire in focused concentration. She walked over to her lab coat hanging in the hallway closet and removed the last page of her research notebook. She sat on the couch and contemplated the serious ramifications of her discovery. Making her decision, Anna stood up and abruptly tore the page into little pieces. With a swift gesture, she threw the scraps containing the answers to the sulphur water serum into the dying fire and watched them catch flame.

The small fireplace emitted a warm glow that turned Anna's skin to gold satin. She turned to switch off the light and proceeded quietly up the stairs to her bedroom.

3

Kate's Mountain Lodge—West Virginia, USA

Meanwhile, an ocean away, thunder roared loudly and rain poured down in steady streams over Greenbrier, West Virginia. The raggedy dog winced and nestled up closer to the large fireplace in the 1918 tavern called Kate's Mountain Lodge. The logs were in full flame, crackling and spitting, emitting a familiar and comfortable aroma.

Seated at a square wooden table next to the fireplace, two middle-aged men were engrossed in low-toned conversation. They were thankful that the harsh weather had emptied the tavern, which otherwise afforded spectacular Allegheny Mountain Range views in every direction. After finishing a dinner of Southern fried chicken with yams, the first man slowly removed his eyeglasses and began cleaning them. The second man picked up his brandy snifter, swirled the golden liquid around and set it back down on the table.

"This is of great concern, and I am honored you have asked me to head up this immense and critical project. Do I understand correctly, there is no ceiling on this budget? We will need an enormous amount of capital to hire the best research scientists and convert the facilities, not to mention the security issues."

The other man nodded, his brow quite furrowed. The seriousness of this matter concerned him deeply.

"Damn it, George, our sources have found germ-storing facilities of the highest caliber, storing bubonic plague, smallpox, tuberculosis, yellow fever and only God knows how many more destructive diseases. We are already getting reports of Nazi experimentation with drugs and germs on Polish prisoners. Berlin has big projects going including tabun, the nerve gas, which means the Japs probably have one, too."

He leaned back in his wheelchair and continued,

"British Intelligence has been as cooperative as can be expected and, if my sources are correct, I suspect the Brits will soon make a preemptive strike against the Germans in the Faroe Islands. Germany is getting two-thirds of their high-grade iron ore for manufacturing from the Swedes, who are helping them to quickly build up their navy and air force capabilities."

Taking a big gulp from his crystal brandy snifter, he continued,

"The 'heavy water' plant in Norway has me concerned too, especially after getting two letters from this fellow Einstein on fission and its potential. Sacks visited me and explained how this atom bomb could potentially be something the Germans are working on. Oh, and then we have this new report of a lethal gas called sarin. Damn it to hell and back again, George, we need this started right away and no one is to know about it!"

George looked directly at his friend.

"Yes, the fission report is definitely of concern. We need the advice of Albert Einstein. Max Planck and many others are leaving Germany. I will immediately start a worldwide search to bring on board the best research scientists to collaborate and work under one facility. Also, I might add, we already have some of the very best. Additionally, Mr. President, you will be pleased with our progress on high-grade penicillin, which hopefully we should be able to mass-produce within a few months." He picked up his brandy snifter and drained the last of the glinting liquid, feeling quite satisfied with this exchange.

President Franklin Delano Roosevelt removed his eye-glasses again to clean them. He looked up at his friend, somewhat absently nodding, and repeated himself out loud. "Yes, I talked with Alex Sacks back in October. I want Frank Knox on this. As The Secretary of the Navy, he should be kept fully informed."

The complications of the matter before him and the work of Fermi and Szilard, who worked together at Columbia to ascertain the feasibility of a nuclear chain reaction, led the President to take immediate action, although he did not mention his concern that perhaps Einstein might be a security risk. Physicists were not always the best politicians.

As both men discussed the project, much was happening in the world to cause them concern. They were well aware that in order for German aggression to continue, the Germans would require more fuel, improved aircraft, more research scientists and more money.

"German need to access the warm water Atlantic ports of Norway, leaves the Scandinavian countries particularly vulnerable, which is of concern to Prime Minister Chamberlain." replied The President.

Nodding, George added,

"There is also talk of the Quantum theories and discoveries at a research Institute in Copenhagen, making those scientists a desirable acquisition by The Kaiser Wilhelm Institute."

A deeply concerned President Roosevelt mandated that all scientists be sworn to secrecy on what was to become known as Project D. The few who were involved had the highest security clearance and were approved directly by the President himself.

The seeds of the project, an immense US Biological Weapons Center, were planted that night. Initiated by FDR and George Merck, president of Merck Pharmaceuticals, it would eventually become one of the deepest wartime secrets, matched only by "The Manhattan Project" for developing the atomic bomb. It would warehouse every possible germ imaginable in a secret warehouse located in Fort Detrick, Maryland.

4

The Greenbrier—West Virginia, USA

The following morning at the Sulphur Springs Spa at The Greenbrier, President Roosevelt was handed a heated towel by one of the spa assistants to dry himself off after his mineral water bath. His physicians had told him that soaking in a hot sulphur mineral spring increased hydrostatic pressure on the body, thereby increasing his blood circulation and cell oxygenation. The increased blood flow also helped to dissolve and eliminate toxins from his body, bringing improved nourishment to vital organs and tissues.

The poster sign on the wall near the baths read:

The trace amounts in this water of carbon dioxide, sulphur, calcium, magnesium, and lithium are absorbed by the body and provide healing effects for body organs, stimulate the immune system, and increase production of endorphins, normalizing gland function.

I need all of the above, thought the President somberly. Somewhat discouraged earlier, his morning soak had eased the constant pain in his legs, while giving him time to collect his thoughts before holding another confidential meeting in his hotel suite at The Greenbrier.

There was a knock on the door. Roosevelt shifted his weight in his wheelchair.

"Come in. Oh, hello there, Bill." He watched as the former powerful New York attorney, now on his team, entered with a commanding stride, his briefcase in one hand and rolled up maps under his other arm.

Colonel William Joseph Donovan entered the Presidential suite. To many he was known as "Wild Bill," a nickname he earned on the football team while at Columbia University.

"Good Morning, Mr. President. A quick update: the French Resistance has helped the Brits crack the enigma code, and the Germans have intercepted British senior Naval Intel codes. I'm afraid we are headed for a second confrontation, Sir."

Donovan pulled out large maps and unrolled them on the table, then proceeded to put his briefcase on the chair, open it and hand the President a seven page document.

Looking most serious, his voice dropped to almost a whisper,

"This came from MI6 via the Naval Attaché at the British Embassy in Oslo. It was anonymously sent, we think, by a German, although the BBC broadcast had to be changed to 'Hullo, heir ist London' as a code in order to receive it. This Oslo report outlines the latest German technical developments, especially the radar equipment. It seems legitimate.

"Additionally, 'The Deuxieme Bureau'—the French military intelligence—has directed three French agents to secretly remove 'heavy water' from the plant in Vemork, Norway."

Roosevelt scanned the document with concern. He looked up at Donovan and nodding his head said,

"I heard the German firm IG, which is a partial owner in the Vemork 'heavy water' plant, had ordered 100kg/month. Norsk Hydro's plant maximum production rate was previously limited to 10kg/month, so it seems clear they are working on this atom bomb project."

This information was critical and the President knew right then that Donovan was correct. Germany was rapidly increasing bomber production levels and machinery for a large scale confrontation. The German air strength was double the Anglo-French total. Moreover, the increasingly barbaric behavior of the Nazis towards German Jews as seen during the already-infamous Kristallnacht (Night of Broken Glass), when the SS went on a rampage destroying Jewish-owned shops and property, illustrated clearly Germany's internal policies. He was already aware of the weak state of American defenses.

Both men were Columbia Law School graduates and their mutual respect and admiration for each other was profound despite their origins in opposing political parties. During Germany's invasion of Poland, Roosevelt had turned to Donovan who had vocally predicted a second major European crisis. On the recommendation of Donovan's friend, Frank Knox, the United States Secretary of the Navy, Roosevelt had given him a number of increasingly important assignments.

Donovan continued,

"The Resistance group in France is gaining some ground. More and more guerilla bands are joining their freedom movement. The Germans are gathering 'heavy water,' deuterium, and materials for bio-germ warfare, as well as stepping up production for their aviation and naval forces. Rechlin, a small town on Lake Muritz north of Berlin is where the Luftwaffe's laboratories and research centers are located."

Donovan moved around the table to lean in closer to the President.

"MI6 British Intelligence is involved in the Special Operations Executive, The SOE, whose sole purpose is to sabotage enemy facilities and collect intelligence throughout Europe. They are working with the Deuxieme Bureau and the Resistance groups to get the 'heavy water' out of Norway."

"So get to the point, Bill." Roosevelt shifted again uncomfortably in his wheelchair. "Do we need to send some of our men over there?"

"Sir, I believe that it would be in the country's best interest to start our own intelligence-gathering system similar to the British MI6 model, and I have two specific men in mind for an initial Intel gathering mission to Paris and Copenhagen."

Doug Conyers was his first pick.

♦　♦　♦　♦　♦　♦　♦　♦　♦　♦

5

Virginia and Washington, DC
April 1940

Flying high above the Chesapeake and Patuxent River, Lieutenant Douglas Conyers, USNR, sat in the cockpit of an experimental Grumman F-4F Wildcat fighter aircraft. Wearing sunglasses with his flight helmet and a flight suit, he exuded the ease and confidence required to fly blithely into the most dangerous of situations. Ruggedly handsome with broad shoulders and dark hair, his sparkling, emerald green eyes hinted at mischief around guys and exuded a smoldering sexuality around women. He glanced occasionally at an old, slightly yellowed black and white photo of a young woman on his instrument panel.

It's just the way the cards were dealt, he thought to himself, feeling a moment of soul-searing hurt.

"A beautiful morning up here," he joked into the microphone attached to his helmet. He executed a flyby at 330 mph, buzzing the control tower and rocking the wings just for fun.

"Get your head out of the clouds and back to the routine," said the lighthearted voice in his headphones. "We need you focused to run those test patterns."

After completing the test patterns, Doug was instructed to run simulated crash landings. He winked at the photo and prepared to perform the required maneuvers by adjusting various switches and knobs on the plane's instrument panel.

"I feel closer to you up here," he whispered to her, after pushing the microphone away from his mouth so it wouldn't broadcast, "but I've got to go back down to earth now."

Doug's fondest memories were of his mother, and he kept her picture in his wallet at all times. It was his good luck token, and he never went flying without tacking it to his instrument panel.

Putting the microphone back to his mouth, he plunged the plane down towards the ocean. He felt exhilarated as he fell, feeling the strange pull of the earth and the inevitable sadness that always struck him when leaving the skies.

After running several test sequences, Doug was ordered to return to the runway. He beamed as he gracefully landed the plane and shut off the engine.

Good show, he thought, as he took off his helmet, roughed up his flattened hair and pushed open the cockpit. *Three hundred and thirty miles per hour—this bird is a taker.* With the swift, spare movement that comes with years of practice, he took his mother's photograph off the instrument panel and tucked it back in his wallet, then quickly pulled his broad-shouldered frame out of the cockpit. The exhilaration and thrill of taking these planes to their max never left him. Seeing the world from a bird's-eye view always gave him a chance think more clearly—away from the crowds and up among the clouds.

As he strode down the tarmac, he saw his friend and fellow aviator, Lenny. Both men had recently been involved in a highly confidential special test program on Catalina Island to undergo special combat, martial arts and counter espionage training.

There, they renewed a friendship that had begun in prep school as youngsters.

"Doug, great barrel roll," Lenny teased, his brown eyes twinkling.

Doug jokingly, in his deep voice, took a well-deserved dig at his pal, whose reputation as a skirt chaser was well known. "Hey, Sir Glad-a-Bag, thanks. How are ya? What are you doing here?"

Lenny laughingly bristled back,

"That would be Sir Galahad to you, pal."

Doug gave Lenny a friendly "hello" slap on the back, then switched subjects quickly.

"Yup, Sir Galahad. He's a great thoroughbred and probably having one hell of a time at the stud farm—I'll bet you one hundred dollars his offspring will win the Derby this year. Speaking of which, how are the gals?" he said with good-natured nonchalance.

Both men were tall, handsome, single and very popular with the ladies.

"Last time we went out on the town together, you went home with the blonde AND the brunette, and I got the redhead, right? It's true what they say about that temper, I discovered," Doug recollected ruefully. "Next time, I get the blonde," he said as he grinned.

Lenny started to make a flip comment regarding studs, but remembered his message. He looked intently at Doug. "We have both just been ordered to headquarters to meet with the top brass."

"Any idea why?" asked Doug in a rather nonchalant fashion.

"I think it might be serious this time," Lenny said with a faint grin.

"The Secretary of the Navy!"

Doug took off his sunglasses, squinting his green eyes in the sunlight,

"You mean Frank Knox?" He looked seriously at Lieutenant Leonard Anderson, both losing their lighthearted demeanors as they proceeded together toward the building to meet with Secretary Knox.

So, it's time, Doug thought to himself, *about time. After all, there isn't much more I can learn doing drills.* He drew himself up, squared his shoulders and marched into the building.

◆   ◆   ◆   ◆   ◆   ◆   ◆   ◆   ◆   ◆

An aide escorted them directly into the Secretary's office, and after shaking hands, both men took a seat in the leather chairs in front of the large mahogany desk.

"Gentlemen, it is my pleasure to inform you that you will both be leaving for Paris immediately. It would seem our German cousins are getting quite frisky. We need a communications network set up in Paris and Copenhagen. Lieutenants Conyers and Anderson, you were hand-selected for outstanding performance during your recent Catalina Island training and for your extensive knowledge of aviation, linguistics and communications. This is highly classified, and as such, you will have top security clearance for this mission.

"Apparently, the Germans have stepped up their production of tabun and other chemical warfare agents. Our British friends report accelerated German activity in Norway with 'heavy water,' increasing the speculation about a German dirty bomb. Rumors of Nazi experiments, injecting the captured Polish people and other inmates with strains of mosquito mucus and yellow fever, are also being reported. MI6 Reports indicate Nazi medical experiments in the work camps are increasing rapidly, along with an outbreak of diphtheria.

"Your mission is to gather as much intelligence as you can and report back immediately. The safety of Americans and our interests overseas could be compromised."

The Secretary put his weathered briefcase on the desk and continued,

"You are to meet with Resistance contacts in Paris, set up safe houses just in case this situation escalates and report back to Washington. Use any means to obtain German aircraft plans, including the new prototypes for the Messerschmitt, troop movements and germ production statistics. Assist our allies in getting top scientists out of Germany and Poland. Your fluency in French and German should prove to be a tremendous asset."

"Inside these envelopes," the Secretary told them, "are instructions detailing your upcoming mission. Everything you need to know is inside. When you are finished reading the instructions—right now—memorize them, give the envelopes back to me, and I will destroy them. No one is to know about this. This directive comes straight from the top. Do I make myself clear?"

Both men nodded solemnly in unison. "Yes sir."

"If, for some reason, you are caught, be aware that since we currently maintain neutral status, we will deny any and all involvement. You are basically on your own. Understood?"

Doug and Lenny nodded that they understood fully.

In silence, the Secretary opened the combination lock on his briefcase, reached in and handed one sealed envelope to Doug, the other to Lenny.

Doug considered his envelope for a second, noting the White House seal, before breaking it and opening the envelope. The heading read 'Highly Classified—Project Delta F.' The letter outlined their mission to meet with operatives in Paris and Copenhagen. They were to build an intelligence communications network by locating and securing a number of safe houses in France in case the war escalated and necessitated the evacuation of Americans. The letter outlined a top secret Oslo report that detailed the Germans were using an R.D.F., a radio direction finding radar system, as well as increased Junker 88 light bomber production to be produced by April.

The Secretary leaned back in his leather chair, assessing each man as they read their instructions. Both had outstanding military records. But he was not sure why Lieutenant Conyers had been called back to active duty especially for this mission. He had been attending MIT for the past year. *Surely they had officers in the ranks who could have been assigned to this mission. Nonetheless, this was Donovan's call. And Conyers, in addition to being an outstanding pilot, had been recognized for his work on radio transmission to accurately locate a bomber's range.* He contemplated this for a moment while watching the men's facial expressions closely. He wanted to wipe that permanent smile off Lieutenant Anderson's face.

As Doug and Lenny finished reading their instructions, they looked up at each other and simultaneously felt the enormity of the task they had just been handed. They also realized the serious ramifications should they fail. Somberly, they each put their instructions back into their envelopes. Slowly, each man handed his envelope back to the Secretary. In sharp contrast, the Secretary quickly turned and threw the two envelopes into the flames of the roaring fire blazing in the fireplace behind him, and watched them burn to ashes.

"You are to pack civilian clothes and leave immediately on a DC-3 bound for Paris via Shannon, Ireland. Good luck, gentlemen. You have been training for this mission. Rest assured that if we did not consider you the best, you would not have been chosen for this assignment."

The Secretary leaned forward and handed them their plane tickets and travel documents in a small pouch, which identified them as American businessmen. Doug and Lenny rose and shook hands with the Secretary, then left his office to head back to pack for their assignment.

6

Copenhagen
April 5, 1940

Early morning in her townhouse, Anna drew her woolen wrap around her more tightly and drained the last of the coffee from her porcelain cup. She set it down carefully on the lace tablecloth covering the kitchen table, a table with room for only two. *But then again*, Anna thought, *there are only two of us.* Anna and her sister Britta were the only residents in this small, immaculately clean two-bedroom townhouse. This was their first independent home since leaving Dr. Cunningham's cottage at Oxford three years ago.

She imagined herself and Britta sharing a cup of coffee and talking before Anna had to leave for work, but most often, Anna sat alone with her thoughts. *Once Britta feels better…today is the day!*

Anna glanced at the small clock over the French doors leading out to a small brick courtyard. It read four-thirty.

I must hurry. Anna placed her coffee cup in the sink. Her gaze strayed outside to the dark road again, where she noticed an old car sitting at the end of the street. *Strange, I didn't notice that car there before,* thought Anna, noticing the trail of cigarette smoke coming from the driver's window. She quickly dismissed it. She had more important things on her mind today.

In Copenhagen, most people rode either the trolley or their bicycles. Anna estimated it would take twenty-five minutes to reach the research lab at Blegdamsvej 17 if they took the trolley. Britta's illness had progressed to the point where she rarely slept through the night without pain, so Anna would ordinarily let her rest. This morning she couldn't afford to waste any time. She walked quickly across the hardwood floor to the bottom of the stairs.

"Britta, wake up. We have to get to the lab." She called.

Britta slowly emerged from her bedroom, and Anna was again saddened by her appearance. Dark haired, with hollowed-out cheeks, the dark circles under Britta's eyes never seemed to fade. She appeared older than her years. Anna was well aware that tomorrow was Britta's twenty-first birthday, but she was also well aware that as Britta's illness progressed, she might not make it through the year.

Anna deeply admired her sister's perseverance in her singing career, knowing the toll it took on Britta's energy. Britta had been blessed with a beautiful sultry voice. More recently, Britta's strength had been diminishing rapidly, and over the last two months, she had not been strong enough to sing at all.

As Anna climbed the stairs, she whispered anxiously,

"Britta, please hurry. I'm willing to risk giving you some of the remaining formula to see if it helps you, but we have to get there before Dr. Spelman arrives. If I am caught, at the very least I will lose my position at the Institute."

Anna's mind wandered to Dr. Spelman, her superior and mentor on the project. She had recently become uncomfortable in his presence, an unsettling intuition that was eroding her trust in his guidance. *Perhaps I am just imagining this*, thought Anna as a chill ran up her spine. Later she would realize just how prophetic her thoughts of this morning actually were.

♦　♦　♦　♦　♦　♦　♦　♦　♦　♦

A half hour later, they arrived at The Niels Bohr Institute after an uneventful trolley ride. Anna took in the unassuming building for a moment, then hastened to get inside with her sister. With her condition worsening by the second, Britta walked extremely slowly.

"You can do it," Anna encouraged softly. Britta nodded, grimaced and forced a weak smile. She gathered up her strength and continued into the Institute and up the stairs with Anna.

The Institute was deserted at this early hour, but Anna looked around nervously anyway as she continued to her lab. She was particularly worried something would backfire while administering the serum to Britta, but it was a calculated risk she was prepared to take. The results of three years' worth of laboratory testing with this sulphur water had proven the miraculous regenerative properties, but now there was precious little of it left. Anna recalled how it had cured Britta's cut as a small child, which reinforced her decision to administer the serum to Britta this morning.

As Anna helped hurry Britta through the lobby, she breathed a sigh of relief mistakenly thinking they had entered the Institute unseen. Unbeknownst to her, Dr. Spelman, who was walking down an adjacent corridor, had spotted them. With suspicious eyes and furrowed brow, he decided to follow them to discover why Anna was there at this early hour, especially with her sister. *It must have something to do with our research*, he thought to himself. However, before following them, he needed to make an urgent phone call.

◆ ◆ ◆ ◆ ◆ ◆ ◆ ◆ ◆ ◆

Once inside the lab, Anna closed the door and hung their coats on a hook. She quietly directed Britta to a stool in front of her lab station. As Britta sat down, Anna noticed the look of fear and uncertainty on her sister's face.

Increasingly silent and somber feelings of doubt had entered Britta's thoughts, stinging her mind. *What if the serum does not work? What if there are side effects? Paralysis? Death?* As each ominous thought entered her mind, Britta felt her resolve rapidly deteriorate.

As if reading Britta's thoughts, Anna smiled at her sister encouragingly. She pulled out a syringe, a small vial containing a clear liquid and a bottle of isopropyl alcohol from the cabinet on top of her lab station. Anna put the needle into the vial and slowly filled the syringe with the serum. Sitting down next to Britta, Anna felt her sister stiffen in fear.

"This will not hurt," she promised.

Britta was not convinced.

"Anna, are you sure this is going to work?" Pulling a ball of cotton from the top drawer of her lab station, Anna doused it with alcohol and then softly rubbed it onto the spot where she would administer the injection into Britta's arm. Britta clenched her teeth in anticipation of the needle's sting. Anna leaned in and kissed Britta's forehead, then injected the serum. Britta squeezed her eyes shut.

"There, all done," smiled Anna. "Everything will be just fine."

Britta glanced at her with apprehension. She wanted to believe her older sister, but she was still afraid.

"It will work," said Anna more firmly.

Suddenly, the door to the lab swung open, startling the two sisters. There stood a glaring Dr. Spelman, whose face displayed a mixture of curiosity and growing anger. Anna glanced quickly at his disheveled appearance, and then instantly dropped the syringe into the open drawer behind her while slipping the vial of remaining serum into her pocket. She prayed he hadn't noticed her actions.

"What is going on here!" he demanded. His face tightened with anger. "You know unauthorized personnel are not allowed in the lab," he added, eyeing Britta. "This is against protocol."

"I'm am so sorry, Dr. Spelman," replied Anna.

"My sister was merely accompanying me before we go to her doctor's appointment this morning. I stopped by to pick up my purse, which I left behind last night. I may not be back today depending on her doctor's recommendation."

Dr. Spelman eyed her curiously, his anger abating somewhat.

Please let him believe me, she nervously thought, though her outside demeanor remained calm. They retrieved their coats and headed for the door. At the far side of the lobby, just as they were about to reach for the door, Anna's heart jumped upon hearing a voice call out her name. She turned quickly to face Dr. Spelman again.

"Yes?" she answered anxiously, her pulse now racing.

"You forgot your purse," he said with a dubious expression. He held up her purse.

Anna hoped her demeanor did not betray her emotions or her longing to leave the Institute hastily as she walked across the lobby to him.

Trying not to tremble, she took her bag from his hand and said, "Thank you."

She turned and walked briskly back to Britta, resisting the urge to look back at Dr. Spelman. Upon reaching Britta, Anna linked her arm through Britta's and they quickly left the Institute. Dr. Spelman stood there a moment longer, contemplating Anna's actions, the peculiar expression on his face still evident.

♦ ♦ ♦ ♦ ♦ ♦ ♦ ♦ ♦ ♦

7

The Research Lab

Dr. Spelman turned and headed directly for the research lab. He entered and sat quietly at Anna's lab station, a look of intense concentration on his face.

What were they doing here? He wondered with a ruthless impatience. He saw Anna's research notebook on the lab station and as he glanced through it, he noticed the last page was torn out.

"A curious thing, to rip out the last page of a research notebook," he mumbled with a stern, unsmiling face. He studied the end of the notes looking for a clue that would indicate what would have been on the missing page. A few minutes later, frustrated and finding nothing, he slammed the notebook down on the lab station.

♦ ♦ ♦ ♦ ♦ ♦ ♦ ♦ ♦ ♦

Dr. Spelman, a renowned molecular biologist, was a man in his mid-fifties, with a diminishing tuft of hair, a stocky build and a slight paunch. He was a domineering, austere scientist, who relentlessly drove himself and those around him to succeed at their tasks. He could verbally cut his subordinates and colleagues to pieces, having complete impatience for failure and incompetence.

One of the top, senior, much-celebrated scientists at The Niels Bohr Institute, his research in the field of X-ray crystallogy, a method used to determine the three-dimensional structures of biomolecules, had paved the way for new and exciting research. It had inspired a new generation of young scientists hoping to further expand on what he had already discovered.

A very vain, cocky Dr. Spelman strode quickly to his office to reflect on the mystery of the missing page. His mind was fraught with questions and seemingly no answers in sight. His thoughts took a dark twist as he considered that Anna might have beaten him to solving the mystery of the sulphur water.

♦ ♦ ♦ ♦ ♦ ♦ ♦ ♦ ♦ ♦

As the years had passed, Dr. Spelman had become completely obsessed with this project. The fame, the acclaim, the money: Dr. Spelman craved it all. He wanted the answer and he wanted it now. And he wanted Anna, too.

As he sat at his desk, he knew it would not be long before THEY came calling. His name and his research were well known. His mind and his genius aptitude in molecular structure were highly sought after in these tumultuous times. Somehow, more than likely through one of the hired researchers at The Kaiser Wilhelm Institute, Hitler had learned of the breakthroughs coming out of The Niels Bohr Institute, making Dr. Spelman a desirable addition to their plans.

As Dr. Spelman gazed out the window in quiet contemplation, the silence was instantly broken by the opening bang of the door, snapping him back to reality, sending his heart slamming hard against the wall of his chest.

♦ ♦ ♦ ♦ ♦ ♦ ♦ ♦ ♦ ♦

Dr. Spelman felt the sweat bead on his forehead. In front of him, two men sat staring at him with the cool, calculating eyes of killers, quite comfortable with their feet up on his desk. His office felt cold to him. A chill ran through him.

"Have you considered our offer?" asked the blonde, steel-eyed man named Lukas.

"I told you already over the phone," insisted Dr. Spelman, "I am not interested."

The blonde man smiled maliciously which showed his front gold tooth, and turned to look at his partner, Finn. Finn was a hideous-looking man with a stocky build and a prominent forehead. His eyes were colorless, displaying no emotion whatsoever. Both men had swastikas tattooed onto their necks as a public display of their loyalty to the party and to Hitler's vision.

"Dr. Spelman, I think you are not fully considering our offer. One million Reichsmarks if you successfully deliver the formula," stated Lukas. "You will also be given special status within the party. Laboratories and research aid, access to more resources than you can possibly imagine and limitless funding. More importantly, you can help us—or you can die. It does not matter to us." Lukas emphasized the latter, as his eyes glinted with malicious delight, watching Dr. Spelman fidget nervously in his chair.

♦ ♦ ♦ ♦ ♦ ♦ ♦ ♦ ♦ ♦

Dr. Spelman became of real interest when the Nazis learned that The Niels Bohr Institute was spearheading not only revolutionary Quantum Mechanics and molecular projects, but also a project run by Dr. Spelman to develop a drug that could cure most diseases and maladies.

The cure-all at this time was penicillin. The miracle drug for effectively combating infection could only be produced at a higher-grade level in incredibly small doses. Only England and the United States currently had access to this high-grade penicillin. Hitler had become increasingly aware of the necessity for research into the fields of biology and medicine. The recruiting of scientists had recently accelerated.

♦ ♦ ♦ ♦ ♦ ♦ ♦ ♦ ♦ ♦

Dr. Spelman considered what Lukas had to offer. He would be a very wealthy man. He would be protected by the

Nazis, and therefore safe from them, solving two of his most imminent problems. The fear in him was palpable as he grabbed his handkerchief from his pocket to mop his brow.

He felt that Anna was lying to him. More than likely, she had found the answer, the elusive master switch, which could shut down the growth and invasion of aggressive destructive cells and reverse any cellular damage. He felt bitterness well up in him. *I should have been the one to solve the mystery.* Was he not one of the most brilliant scientists in his field, if not the world?

He also felt the usual emptiness. With Nazi resources, he would become a great and powerful man. He could fulfill all his desires.

"Dr. Spelman, we do not wish to resort to such methods as brute force, but let us be clear. You will get this formula for us. You will get it or risk the suffering and torture of those closest to you, your female colleague and yourself included. We are through being polite. It is a courtesy we extend to very few," said Lukas with a menacing tone.

His calm, deliberate delivery made the message sound all the more ominous.

Beside Lukas, Finn sat up straighter, his muscles flexing. Dr. Spelman quaked in his seat, desperately trying to maintain a semblance of outer calm.

"The one million Reichmarks," began Dr. Spelman, "will be placed in the bank account we have discussed?"

"Yes," responded Lukas. "When you deliver the formula, we will give you the account number."

Dr. Spelman nodded, but remained silent.

"Well, I believe we have worn out our welcome. Hopefully, for your sake, the next time we meet, you will bring us something useful," laughed Lukas, as he stamped out his cigarette on Dr. Spelman's desk, burning a small, black hole in the wood. Slowly Finn and Lukas rose to leave.

As they left, Dr. Spelman sank into his chair, shaken and scared. He glanced at Anna's research notebook. His fear and desire were beginning to outweigh the guilt.

"Better to be rich than dead," he thought as he rose to leave. Before exiting his office, he stopped at a filing cabinet and rifled through the drawers. He pulled out a file with Anna's name. Finding the information he was after, he wrote it down on a piece of paper and headed for the door.

♦ ♦ ♦ ♦ ♦ ♦ ♦ ♦ ♦ ♦

8

Annapolis, Maryland
First Week in April

"Come on, Doug, let's get our bags packed and get going. A few days in Paris, great French wines and l'amour with a pit stop in Ireland for some good Irish whiskey and loveable lasses, then a stop in Copenhagen with beautiful Scandinavian girls—maybe we'll get laid—what could be better than that?" said Lenny laughing, although he understood the danger and importance of their mission. He headed down the hallway, his duffle bag slung over his shoulder.

"Is that all you think about?" Doug yelled after him, although, admittedly, Lenny did have a way of rephrasing the mission to make it sound very appealing, more like a pleasurable vacation. *It's all in the positioning of your mind and how you think about things*, contemplated Doug, shrugging.

Unusually somber, Doug sat on the edge of his bed and considered his orders. Doug knew that their instructions came directly from Colonel Donovan with President Roosevelt's full approval. He quickly proceeded to pack a bag with a variety of shirts and slacks and go through his mail, stacked on the small bedside table.

"Another Sears and Roebuck catalog, and more bills," he muttered.

But one letter stood out—an ivory envelope postmarked three weeks ago from Copenhagen. It appeared to be a personal note. The return address was from a Dr. Johann Cunningham—not a name he recognized, but Johann meant John in Dutch and Slavic languages. Shoving the note in his inside jacket pocket, he figured he would have plenty of time to read it on the flight. He was not looking forward to the many hours in the air on a civilian flight—he liked flying best when he was in the pilot's seat.

However, the pit stop for the refueling and servicing of the DC-3 in Shannon, Ireland, would make up for it. He would have a chance to see Mickey O'Grady, the thoroughbred trainer, and the new foal sired by a stallion in which he had a small financial interest. "The Sport of Kings" was one of Doug's true passions—thoroughbred racing and breeding horses.

Lenny entered Doug's room without knocking.

"You ready, pal? They actually sent a car and driver to take us to the airport—no doubt to make sure we get on the plane," he said, grinning.

As they left the room, Doug took a long look around, glanced at the framed picture of his mother and closed the door quietly. As they exited the building, both men got in the car and were whisked to the Washington airport.

9

Pan Am Flight to Shannon, Ireland
April 6th 1940

Doug and Lenny were weary after hours of flying. They tried to sleep on the turbulent Pan American flight from the United States to Europe.

"How long have we been flying, Doug?" asked a waking Lenny with a big yawn, rubbing his eyes and feeling his ears pop from the pressure. He looked over Doug and out the window.

"I lost count many hours ago. This plane only has a top speed of two hundred thirty-seven miles per hour," groaned Doug. "This is a far cry from what we usually fly, Lenny," Doug remarked.

"We can't be too far now from landing in Ireland," he said, "so tell me about this O'Grady guy we are meeting in Shannon?"

Doug responded,

"I have a share in a horse called Beau Geste, a two-year-old colt that O'Grady had been training. I struck up a friendship with O'Grady a few years ago while visiting the racetrack in Saratoga Springs for the Fasig-Tipton sale of thoroughbreds."

Doug continued,

"O'Grady pointed out to me the similarities between thoroughbreds and humans. He explained that even though genetics and bloodlines play a big part with these horses, a thoroughbred is trained from the beginning to win. A good trainer is essential in encouraging the best performance, and these thoroughbreds are exceptional athletes. Horses, like humans, have good days and bad days and preferences, like preferring to run on a wet track or a dry track. They are trained for hours to get in the starting gate, much the same way pilots like us are trained to sit in the cockpit of a plane; both are exercises required for space-restricting conditioning. I learned a lot from him."

Lenny said,

"Sounds like quite the fellow. I'm sure I'll like him. Right now, I'm having a bad day trying to sleep on this damn flight. You would think Washington could have given us more notice. I had a date tonight." He leaned back in his seat, grunted and closed his eyes for another snooze.

Doug settled back into his window seat trying to stop the constant chatter in his brain as he retrieved the note from Dr. Cunningham from his jacket pocket. As he pulled the ivory note out of the envelope, he noted the embossed letter "C" at the top of the note.

Dear Douglas, by way of introduction, I knew your mother many years ago in Germany before you were born…

Reading the note, Doug was immediately intrigued by the vagueness of it and began to feel an underlying trepidation. He sensed there was more to this note, more on what was not said rather than by what was said.

Doug was confused by this as his mother passed away when he was still a young boy, and he did not remember any mention of that name. However, eternally curious, Doug decided when he got to Copenhagen, he would accept Dr. Cunningham's offer to visit.

Doug looked at Lenny, now snoring with a smile on his face- that permanent smile that tricked most into misjudging both his ability and his tenacity. Doug knew that Lenny had displayed a mischievous, impertinent bend at West Point coupled with a furious, sometimes uncontrolled temper. He saved his charm for his superiors. Doug had already seen that temper as they had gone to high school for one year together. Doug had saved his ass on the football team when the team went to beat up on Lenny after one of their games. Lenny had been pulled out of their private boarding school, and sent to a public school in the Bronx. The Depression had wiped out Lenny's family's fortune.

I guess I can't blame Lenny for not wanting to talk about it, after all his father's suicide was on the front page of the newspapers. Doug leaned back and closed his eyes for the rest of the flight.

♦ ♦ ♦ ♦ ♦ ♦ ♦ ♦ ♦ ♦

The plane finally landed at the Shannon Airport, and as they disembarked, Doug and Lenny separated from the other passengers and made their way to the front of the airport terminal. A lorry pulled up, driven by O'Grady, who was the trainer and owner of the highly successful "Starry Way Thoroughbred Stables" located outside of Shannon. O'Grady greeted them warmly, slapping Doug on the back.

"So, who do you like in the Derby?" O'Grady asked, grinning widely. It was April and the much-anticipated Kentucky Derby thoroughbred race was the first weekend in May at Churchill Downs in Kentucky, only four weeks away. Grabbing their luggage, O'Grady loaded it into the truck, while Doug and Lenny jumped in the front for the short ride out to the stables; the men discussed the Triple Crown.

♦ ♦ ♦ ♦ ♦ ♦ ♦ ♦ ♦ ♦

All winners have great trainers, Doug thought early on, and O'Grady was one of the very best. O'Grady conversely saw the honest determination in Doug's character; he was the type of man that other men would follow without question, "a man's man." Throughout the years, O'Grady had counseled Doug on investing in a few horses that he felt had great potential.

O'Grady, increasingly well known in Europe for breeding good thoroughbreds had thereby gained access to the royalty of Europe, as well as to the rich and famous. Once the Nazi regime began buying more horses, British Intelligence had approached O'Grady for help in getting information out of Germany. He was happy to oblige.

◆　◆　◆　◆　◆　◆　◆　◆　◆　◆

Upon their arrival at the stables, the men walked around to view the new foals and get caught up. Doug inhaled deeply the fresh smell of grass and hay. It was invigorating after being cooped up inside an airplane for hours. They paused beside an open stable door to watch a young groom—a tall, lanky boy of ten or eleven years old named Sean—put a bridle on a mare that O'Grady had just brought back from Germany.

Suddenly, the mare reared up, striking Sean and knocking him to the ground. Doug realized the boy was in imminent danger of being trampled by the panicked horse. Instinctively, he raced into the stall and grabbed the injured boy from beneath the hooves of the bucking horse, receiving a blow from a flailing hoof himself at the same time. O'Grady raced in and secured the mare while Doug carried the injured boy outside. Lenny took one look at them and asked O'Grady where the nearest hospital was, realizing that Doug and Sean would both require stitches.

"Well, the closest would be our vet for thoroughbreds. He's good. So don't worry, this doesn't look too serious," replied O'Grady. "I have seen many jockey accidents in my lifetime," gently chuckling as he closed the door to the stall. "In fact, he is on the grounds. He was going to perform a simple procedure on this mare."

Doug scooped up young Sean carefully in his arms and carried him to the vet. "Don't worry, son. We'll have you fixed up in no time at all."

Sean looked up at Lieutenant Doug Conyers and smiled, reassured. As he looked at Doug's bleeding head, he was in awe of this man who had pulled him out from under the horse's hooves. *He never even considered his own danger to rescue me*, thought Sean, instantly idolizing the American.

When they arrived at the stable's clinic, the vet took Sean into an examining room and tended to the injured boy. While the vet was tending to Sean, O'Grady sat on the bench outside the door and told Doug and Lenny,

"Sean came to live at the stables. His parents were killed in an automobile accident when he was very young, and he was then placed in foster care. He bounced from foster home to foster home. Finally, he ran away. After finding him hiding in the hayloft for the fifth time, my wife and I, being childless, adopted him. Sean displayed a natural talent for horses. He has been a blessing to us."

Doug formed an instant connection and liking for the young boy. He understood how it was for a boy to lose his parents at a young age.

"O'Grady, you are a good man. I knew I liked you before, but taking Sean in is proof that you are also a compassionate human being. I like the kid; he didn't even cry and I know that cut has to hurt like hell. Mine sure does," Doug said with a grimace, while he held an icepack wrapped in a white towel to the cut on the side of his head.

A half hour later, the vet emerged with good news.

"Sean has not been seriously hurt and only needed a few stitches. He will have the use of his arm back in no time Keep him off the horses for a while, no working out on the track with the other work boys for at least two weeks." He instructed O'Grady, "Put Sean to bed for a good night's rest when you get home because I have given him a mild sedative. He should sleep comfortably through the night, perhaps you should teach him to drive the stable hay truck instead."

Chuckling, the vet now turned his attention to the cut on Doug's head. Doug sat on the edge of an examining table, still feeling slightly disoriented. Lenny, a look of humor on his face, stood at Doug's side as the doctor stitched him up.

"Remember when you sprained your ankle during football practice in high school?" said Lenny, with audible good humor. "You must just be accident-prone and very, very fragile to need stitches from a little banging of your head on a hoof," he said jokingly.

Fragile would hardly be a word that anyone would use to describe Douglas Conyers. Doug looked at him with a scowl on his face, and Lenny began to laugh.

"Okay," said the vet, "all stitched up. You'll be fine—get a good night's sleep and here is an extra bandage. Change it in the morning. I'll have a quick look at Sean first thing tomorrow when I return to the stables."

"Will do, and thanks, Doc," Doug said.

O'Grady asked,

"Lenny, would you be so kind as to take Sean back to the house? Sean, will you ask Mom to start dinner? We will be along shortly."

Lenny and Sean left for the house.

O'Grady turned to Doug.

"Lad, thanks for saving the boy's life. We've had some temper problems with this mare ever since we purchased her in Germany. Maybe she wasn't happy about the info she carried. We've smuggled some great aviation plans out of Germany in her. By the way, how well do you know this Lenny character?"

"Lenny and I went to Phillips Academy many years ago, and we played football together on the school team. But his family lost their entire fortune during the Depression. He had to drop out of school. There were some rumors about his father committing suicide and something equally tragic regarding his mother, but I don't remember the details. By coincidence, we ended up years later in the same survival and intelligence training program at Catalina."

O'Grady turned to Doug and in a most serious tone asked,

"Do you trust him?"

"I don't have any reason not to trust him. We were both handed instructions by the White House in sealed envelopes. I'm sure the directive came directly from Roosevelt and Donovan. We have to leave for Paris in a few hours, and I need a contact from you. Someone that you trust that can help us set up safe houses in case the war escalates."

"Absolutely, my friend, I have just the man: his name is Jacques Dumas."

♦ ♦ ♦ ♦ ♦ ♦ ♦ ♦ ♦ ♦

Kathleen, O'Grady's wife of fifteen years, put an exhausted young Sean to bed when they arrived back home. The O'Grady house was an old stone farmhouse with many bedrooms and a large, inviting kitchen, which was warmed by the brightly burning fire in the hearth. Kathleen, her thick brown hair in a long braid, swung a pot out from over the fire where it had been slowly cooking all day, removed the lid and ladled out her famous lamb stew into three bowls. She placed the stew on the table along with freshly baked Irish soda bread, churned butter, and a jug of ale.

As the men started eating dinner, Doug and Lenny listened intently as O'Grady filled them in on his recent travels to Germany, France and Belgium where he had been selling and racing thoroughbreds. Being a thoroughbred owner and trainer made an ideal cover for O'Grady as one of the members of the European intelligence and resistance community. O'Grady shared the latest news from Europe with them.

♦ ♦ ♦ ♦ ♦ ♦ ♦ ♦ ♦ ♦

O'Grady, between bites of food, continued.

"A few months ago on November 9th, the Sicherheitsdienst, sister agency to the better known Gestapo, captured two British SIS agents at the Café Backus in the Dutch town of Venlo, eight kilometers from the German border. Heinrich Himmler ordered the British spies captured. Hitler will use this as an excuse to claim that The Netherlands was involved with Britain and had violated its own neutrality."

He put down his fork and looked at both men.

"Lads, mark my words: there will be a war with Holland."

He continued with Doug and Lenny's full attention.

"The two British agents were abducted and smuggled back into Germany, then tortured on Himmler's orders. The bad news is that one of them was foolish enough to have a book on him with the names of other agents—quite an embarrassing situation for the Brits—so now Himmler is on a little hunting expedition, and making it more difficult to get Luftwaffe technology plans and their new torpedo types out."

"I do not have a good feeling about this little expedition of ours. At least you got the latest aviation plans out, and inside the horses no less. That was brilliant!" commented Doug, his green eyes clouding over as he looked at the plans spread out on the table.

Almost immediately, the smile left Doug's face. There was a brooding silence as the men reflected on the reality of another European war looming on the very near horizon.

Doug commented,

"The Air Corps has increased its expansion plans to seven thousand pilots per year and forty one groups and I expect that number will soon double."

"President Roosevelt met with our US Ambassador to France, William Bullitt, in October, he has confirmed Hitler's unrelenting territorial nature especially in view of The Munich

Crisis and the Czech Sudetenland occupation." added Lenny fidgeting with his fork. "Germany has an air strength double the Anglo-French total" he said quickly, looking over at Doug for affirmation, knowing the information he just shared was publicly related by President Roosevelt on November 14th.

Hungry and exhausted from their long flight, the men finished the delicious meal that Kathleen had cooked and prepared to return to the airport.

After dinner, O'Grady handed Doug a piece of paper with a Parisian address: 5 Rue Daunou.

"5 Rue Daunou? That's the address of Harry's Bar. Are you kidding?"

"Joking? Not on your life. Come on, let's get you to the airport. I'll get a message to Paris for you."

O'Grady explained the code word that would identify their French contact at the address. They talked for a few more minutes about the situation in Europe, and then got their bags for the trip back to Shannon for the flight to Paris.

Doug and Lenny profusely complimented and thanked Kathleen for dinner so many times that she finally stopped them and laughing said,

"Enough lads. Be on your way now. I have heard more than enough blarney from Mr. O'Grady."

10

Copenhagen—Later that Morning—Jewelers
April 5, 1940

Hurrying home following their visit to the Institute, Anna decided to make a quick stop at the local jewelers. They knocked loudly on the simple wooden door, and waited impatiently for a few minutes.

"Who's there?" replied the scratchy voice of an older man.

"So sorry to wake you up" said Anna as the older man opened the door slowly to let them in. They proceeded to approach the counter of the small, quaint boutique.

"I have an urgent and unusual request," Anna said to the white-haired man, now standing behind the counter.

The jeweler, a kindly looking elderly man with spectacles, replied with a twinkle in his eye,

"And what can I do for you this early morning that would seem so strange?"

Anna pulled out a ruble from her pocket.

"I wonder if you could slice this in half and hollow out the inside for me."

The jeweler looked curiously at her.

"Of course, I suppose I could do that." As he carefully inspected the coin, he told her, "You do realize, my dear, that this is quite valuable because of the askew relief of Nicholas II. Are you sure you want to do this?" he asked softly, realizing she wanted to conceal some secret from the world.

"Yes, I am quite sure," replied Anna, nervously glancing at the clock behind him.

"Can you do it now, please?"

Just then he noticed the small Star of David pendant around her neck and smiled. He nodded, believing he understood the reason for her strange request. *Intelligent young lady, this one is. Who would think to look for a Star of David pendant inside a ruble? But it isn't a Star of David really, is it?* he thought, looking more closely. *This Star of David only has five points, not six. It must be a pentacle that represents the five books of Moses.*

"Now?" exclaimed the jeweler, somewhat surprised by her haste. The jeweler pulled Anna aside for a moment to ask her a question in a low voice. Anna nodded her head yes and handed him the second ruble. Britta was off in another part of the shop, looking at the jewelry displays.

"Yes, my sister and I will wait," responded Anna in a voice loud enough for Britta to hear.

While Anna was waiting, the jeweler pointed out a beautiful, small, intricate music box in the store window. She picked up the music box and opened the top. It played a lovely soft melody.

"Britta, listen to this," said Anna, noticing that Britta was looking very pale.

"Do you remember Mama singing us to sleep with this melody?"

Britta shook her head and said,

"Anna, let's go. I don't feel good," as she reached for the handle of the door to leave.

"Just one moment, Britta. Let me pay for this and then we'll go straight home."

Enchanted, Anna thanked the jeweler and paid for the music box along with the charge for her newly hollowed-out coins. Concerned over Britta's nausea, Anna hailed a taxi to get home as soon as possible.

Anna opened the bag from the jewelry store and slipped the coins in her pocket as she swiftly put a tired Britta to bed. She then hastened to her room to retrieve the microfilm from inside her bra and pulled out the music box she had just bought from the jeweler. Looking at the microfilm, she contemplated it quietly, hardly believing the enormity of the importance contained in this small bit of film. She took the hollowed-out coins from her pocket and placed the film inside one of them. She then removed the vial of serum from her pocket and placed it and the rubles inside the secret compartment in the music box that the jeweler had shown her. She placed the music box in a shoebox and hid it under a loose floorboard under her bed, and then headed to check on Britta to see if the nausea had passed and if she wanted to eat lunch. Anna was relieved to see Britta sleeping peacefully.

◆ ◆ ◆ ◆ ◆ ◆ ◆ ◆ ◆ ◆

Later that night, Britta awoke with a fever and in intense pain. Anna sat next to her and gently placed a cold compress on her forehead. Britta lifted herself up onto her elbows in an attempt to alleviate the pain, but only caused herself more distress. She screamed as the pain shot through her entire body.

"This is a predictable side effect," explained Anna softly. "It will get better, I promise," she said as sobs clogged her throat.

About to cry, Anna retreated downstairs to the sitting room, emotionally drained. She sat and looked out the window, her right cheek comfortably nestled in the palm of her right hand, while the fingers of her left hand tapped soundlessly on the wooden table. Anna saw trails of cigarette smoke coming out of a car window at the end of the street. *There is that car again. I'll have to inquire about it tomorrow,* she reminded herself as her thoughts returned to Britta. Every now and then, she heard a muffled sob from Britta upstairs that would make her heart contract.

Had she made the right choice? What if she had not? In her heart, Anna knew her sister would be all right, but she could barely stand to see her sister in such intense agony. After a while, Anna went into Britta's room to make sure she was all right.

Britta, drained, looked up at her.

"Please, Anna, tell me the frog story again."

Anna glanced at her anxiously, Britta looked tired and pale.

Anna was quiet for a moment and then began her tale. It was the same story she had been telling Britta since she was a little girl.

"Tell me what the sulphur water does again," demanded Britta adamantly.

Anna began the story of a pagan ritual described in their mother's notebook that started at the Russian sulphur spring many years ago.

"Britta, when I was ten, shortly before you were born, I loved to explore the forest near the sulphur spring. It was where Mama collected her herbs for medicinal purposes. I was walking uneasily, checking my balance, along a stone wall in the countryside of our small town in Russia. I continued along the wall, slowly moving away from the town. I thought I might find Mama there collecting her curcina longo plants along with her milk thistle.

"Along the way I found a frog of the most unusual shade of blue. He also had a large growth on his head. I picked him up and put him in my smock pocket.

"I must have taken a wrong path because I accidentally stumbled upon a place I had never been to before: a small, hot sulphur spring surrounded by dense forest. Close by I noticed a round circle with a five-point pentacle drawn in the dirt. I thought it was another child's drawing in the sand, so I jumped inside it, like a hopscotch game. It was quickly growing dark out and the large, rising full moon was a slight shade of pink. I have never seen such a large pink moon."

Anna glanced over at a sleepy Britta and continued.

"I wanted to give the frog a drink of water, so I went over to the spring and dipped my hand in it. It was warm and soothing. As I dipped the frog in the water, it tried to jump out of my hands, but I held on to him tightly. I continued to dip the frog in the sulphur spring."

Anna took a deep breath.

"As I kept dipping the frog in the water of the sulphur spring, the frog's tumor almost completely disappeared. Suddenly, out of nowhere I heard voices echo:

'Goddess of the Moon, from the darkest deep of time, let us drink this miraculous water, and under your powerful moonbeams become divine.'

Glancing towards the forest, I saw a group of adults holding hands in a circle, all chanting the same verse five times under the full moon. They were standing inside my hopscotch circle. Something inside me was afraid. Maybe I was seeing something forbidden.

Terrified, I turned and ran back home, hoping I escaped undetected. I was too afraid to tell Mama or Papa. Surely Papa would have been furious with me for going out so far alone. Years later, I found this quotation inside Mama's notebook containing medicinal remedies along with a picture of a triangle."

Britta nodded with her head resting on the pillow

"I remember seeing that notebook".

"After you were born, Mama and I would take you every day to the sulphur spring to help your cough and ease the pain. Mama believed that this water from deep inside the earth had magical curing properties. It is this sulphur water that I put in vials and took to Oxford with me. It wasn't until last night that I figured out how to recreate this water to restore damaged cells. Britta, this must be *our* secret! There are people out there that would use it for evil purposes."

Anna glanced over at Britta who was now sound asleep. As she turned to leave the room and switch off the light, she noticed a box of matches inscribed in Russian on the night table.

11

Copenhagen
Evening of April 5, 1940

Later that night, Anna retrieved the shoebox from under her bed and opened the small music box. She smiled as she heard the familiar beautiful melody play.

It's wonderful how music can be so comforting. It takes me back to my earlier days, thought Anna.

Anna sat at the edge of her bed in her room gently caressing the rubles, engrossed in very serious thought. She knew the microfilm inside, the final instructions to complete the formula, were the most sacred symbols she had ever written down.

Anna took out the one ruble on which the jeweler had soldered a small gold loop and threaded a small gold chain through it. She placed it alongside the tiny vial of serum in the concealed compartment of the music box that the jeweler had shown her. She returned the shoebox to its place under the loose floorboard beneath her bed.

I need to remember to share the location of the music box with Britta when she is feeling better.

Fatigued, Anna decided to wash up before settling down to sleep. Walking towards the bathroom, she stopped for a moment in front of her dresser and opened the bureau drawer. Anna selected a white cotton chemise, pulled it on and paused to brush her long, blonde hair. She moved into the bathroom and stood, looking into the mirror above the sink. She stared at herself. With her finger, she traced her lips.

They have not been touched in so long, she thought to herself. *I have been so busy caring for Britta and working, I have forgotten to take care of myself.* She gazed at her reflection. An overwhelming sense of responsibility and loneliness took over as the tears flowed freely down her face.

She whispered softly to herself, "There is only Britta that I can trust." She turned off the light, her image fading as the light left the room.

♦ ♦ ♦ ♦ ♦ ♦ ♦ ♦ ♦ ♦

She awakened later that night with a start, perspiration clinging to her white cotton chemise. Anna had yet another dream of moonlit rituals that was shattered by an overpowering bolt of fear.

What am I so afraid of? she thought as she looked over at the journal on her night table with a five-star picture on the cover.

Her mother's belief was that this world contained a natural healing remedy for all ailments. Consumed by her passion to find a cure for her younger daughter's rare illness, she frequently canvassed the forest for rare herbs and plant species. She meticulously documented the medicinal recipes that she developed in a leather-bound journal.

Anna picked up her mother's journal and began to read.

♦ ♦ ♦ ♦ ♦ ♦ ♦ ♦ ♦ ♦

12

Copenhagen—Early Morning at the Institute
April 6th

The next morning, Anna returned to work. It seemed odd to do something so routine in such a life-changing week. As soon as she entered the lab, an assistant informed her that Dr. Spelman had finished his morning meeting and wished to speak with her.

Surely, he doesn't know, she thought as she made her way to his office.

As she stepped inside, she saw Dr. Spelman seated at his desk.

"You may have a seat if you wish," he said to her impatiently after she had been standing a moment too long.

"Of course, thank you," she replied, slightly flustered.

"I was hoping we could talk about the formula that we have been working on for a long time now." He bridled at the distant, clinical look she gave him.

Anna knew she could not tell him she had discovered the last link. She also knew he had a keen understanding of the formula and, in fact, held her research notebook in his hand. She eyed him carefully, preparing herself to lie.

"I have come to the conclusion that we have hit an insurmountable obstacle in our research," she said with conviction, "a wall we will never be able to breach."

Dr. Spelman eyed her with suspicion. He had already considered that she might lie to him; however, he could not be one hundred percent sure. He had no proof. Anna was usually so optimistic in her research, even when faced with difficult challenges and frustrating results. He suspected the sister, whom he knew to be fatally ill, had something to do with this.

"You are usually so optimistic," he commented, as he eyed her with rising irritation.

"I usually am, but I am discouraged," she replied.

"When faced with the overwhelming evidence that we are nowhere near a breakthrough, I am just being practical. I don't think that the discovery of a formula that can restore damaged cells to their normal original state will happen in our lifetime, Dr. Spelman. Nature, with her sophisticated forms of chemistry of living matter, still understands and utilizes methods that we do not yet know how to recreate. However, if you wish, I will continue to work on the molecular mathematical sequencing."

He studied her again quietly. He decided she was lying, but he did not understand why.

13

Paris, France
April 6th

Arriving at Le Bourget Airport in Paris, Doug and Lenny grabbed their bags and hailed a taxi to take them to their rendezvous.

"Connaissez-vous le 5 Rue Daunou, s'il vous plait ?" Doug instructed the driver in perfect French, which he had learned at an early age from his mother.

Doug gazed out the window as they zipped past all the sights. The enormity of this mission weighed heavily on his shoulders, although he knew this was what he was trained to do. His elite training and knowledge, as well as his talent with languages and his technical skills, had all prepared him for this mission. As the taxi screeched to a halt at its destination, Doug was thrown out of his reverie. Lenny glanced at him.

"You daydreamin' there, partner?" said Lenny, smiling, nudging Doug with his elbow.

They stepped out of the taxi as the driver placed their bags on the sidewalk in front of their destination, Harry's Bar—a well-known watering hole and frequent destination for Hemingway, Scott Fitzgerald, Gershwin, Jack Dempsey, Marlene Dietrich, Steinbeck and many other expats. Harry's originated years ago when a successful American jockey, Todd Sloan, familiar to the French racing world, joined a New York saloon owner named Clancey to open up the bar. Harry's Bar was famous for its creation of the drinks "Bloody Mary" and "The Sidecar," conceived between 1915 and 1939.

Once inside Harry's, Doug and Lenny found a secluded table and ordered drinks. Doug leaned back against the mahogany wall, taking in the shields of dark wood bearing the insignia of American colleges and British universities. He intuitively scanned the room looking for the likely contact. It was not long before an imposing individual with dark hair, a lean build and an eye-catching moustache approached their table. To complete the look, the individual had a red scarf tied around his neck. He extended his hand.

"Hemingway?"

O'Grady had given this coded introduction to Doug.

"Froggy, I presume?" Doug responded as instructed.

Doug and Lenny introduced themselves to Jacques Dumas, the French Resistance contact. On first glance, he looked quite ordinary, someone who perhaps could pass as an artist in Montmartre. His English was good, although laced with a thick French accent. After they exchanged the initial pleasantries and ordered food, Dumas got down to business. "I hear we have a mutual friend in Ireland; tomorrow, I will take you on a tour that will assist with communications."

Dumas waited for the waiter to leave before continuing in a low voice. "The Resistance has learned that architects have been hired to produce blueprints for a concentration camp in Silesia, complete with large crematoriums. There are also reports of the gassing of Poles."

Although initially Dumas had a rather pugnacious attitude, a favorable rapport and a trust was quickly established between the three men.

♦ ♦ ♦ ♦ ♦ ♦ ♦ ♦ ♦ ♦

Later that night in his Paris hotel room, Doug tossed and turned in his bed, dreaming of his childhood in 1920s rural

Virginia: He is lying on the grass in front of his home on a sunny and clear day. He is playing alone with tiny, metal toy soldiers. He looks in the distance and sees his mother, hanging linens on a clothesline. The wind begins to pick up, and overhead a flock of birds is flying freely in the darkened sky. Ominous clouds are approaching in the distance. He continues to play, ignoring the warning of the wind.

A few minutes later, the intensity of the wind causes goose bumps to spread over his body and the eight-year-old Douglas gets an uneasy feeling. Suddenly scared, he gets up and runs to his mother to be comforted. He noticed his mother falling, pulling the linens with her as she fell to the ground. He runs to her and kneels beside her.

"Mommy, Mommy, get up." He shakes her arm to get her attention, but her eyes stare motionless at the dark clouds overhead. Doug realizes something is terribly wrong, but he doesn't know what to do. He does not understand why she won't get up.

◆ ◆ ◆ ◆ ◆ ◆ ◆ ◆ ◆

With a jolt, Doug awoke from his nightmare. He looked around the room, his heart pounding as his eyes adjusted to the dark.

"I'm in Paris," he remembered with relief, remembering the time change from the US. A hasty look at the clock and Doug saw that it was three-thirty AM. His forehead and chest were damp with sweat. After a few moments, he began to calm down. He turned over to go back to sleep. He heard Lenny's hotel room door close next door. *Crazy guy must have gone out on the town*, he thought.

As usual, he slept on only one side of the bed. In the quiet, dark stillness of the hotel room, he gazed at the empty side, steeped in loneliness until he finally managed to drift back to sleep.

Doug and Lenny were due to tour one of the safe houses with Jacques Dumas, the Resistance leader, early that morning.

Doug was impressed with Dumas. He would have to remember to thank O'Grady for the contact.

14

Paris
Morning of April 7th

The next morning Doug and Lenny met in the hotel lobby for their appointment with Jacques Dumas who was in charge of the French Resistance, which was predominantly rural guerilla bands in France held together by a passion for freedom. A fastidious leader of men and characterized by fervent emotion, he had succeeded in weaving an ardent and enthusiastic web of connections throughout Europe. The feisty Dumas had earned the loyalty and trust of his men who appreciated his expeditious manner and his carefully executed strategies.

At precisely 0900 in front of the hotel, Dumas drove up in a dirty, old, blue Peugeot car. He got out of the car leaving the engine running and greeted Doug and Lenny, handing them a bag of freshly baked croissants, as he walked around to open the passenger door.

"Bon Matin, Messieurs," he said congenially as he approached with a broad smile. "I trust we can discuss matters in more confidential detail when we arrive at our destination," Dumas said in heavily accented English as Doug got in the front seat and Lenny in the back. They drove off with a screech of wheels.

Dumas easily shifted gears and maneuvered the car at racing speed away from the busy streets of Paris, which gave way to the expansive, colorful countryside. Dumas, quiet until now, started to explain the history of their destination.

"Paris is made up of twenty arrondissments. One of our proposed safe houses is just slightly outside of the city adjacent to a small village. It is a chateau, which has been in use for the last hundred years as a convent for cloistered nuns who have taken a vow of silence. The half-brother of William the Conqueror, otherwise known as William the Bastard, originally built this chateau. History has documented Louis XVI and Marie Antoinette as frequent visitors here. Apparently, it was quite useful during the revolution.

"We are proposing to use this chateau as a communication center with British Intelligence in Gibraltar. Originally, the chateau connected to a vast system of tunnels that underlie Paris. The tunnels are a labyrinth, weaving more than three hundred feet beneath the city, although most of these passageways are closed off now."

They arrived at the imposing chateau, an elegant estate set apart from a small country village at least forty-five minutes from the outskirts of Paris. The car slowly pulled into the long, tree-lined driveway passing through the open high, wrought-iron gate that guarded the property. The chateau, surrounded by formal colorful gardens, was displaying the first signs of spring bloom.

"We need to find someplace quiet to discuss the business at hand," said Dumas quite seriously as they exited the car and made their way up the heather-lined walkway. Dumas knocked loudly on the ornately carved wooden door. They waited patiently at the entrance until a small nun opened the door, bowed her head and retreated silently.

As they entered into the foyer of the chateau, Dumas, looking at Lenny and Doug, said,

"Since she has taken a vow of silence, she is forbidden to talk. Some of these women take the vow at age thirteen and never talk. Imagine that, my friends, a woman who doesn't talk—every man's dream."

Dumas grinned mischievously while twirling his mustache. Dumas led them into an exquisite wood-paneled study, lined with antique leather-bound books and a large marble fireplace. To the right was an expansive window reaching from the floor to the ceiling. The heavy, dark-green, damask drapery was tied back, giving the whole room an air of regal elegance. Placed in front of the fireplace was an intricate Persian rug and a large mahogany desk.

It was strangely quiet and Dumas explained that the nuns spent most of their time in the chateau chapel praying, which made this an ideal safe house. Dumas strode across the inlaid wooden floor, over to the intricately paneled bookcase.

Doug was eyeing the fantastic number of leather-bound books: Shakespeare, Socrates, HG Wells, James Joyce, Edith Wharton, Carl Jung, Robert Frost, Aristotle, the titles went on and on. "Wow," he commented enthusiastically, "I could spend an entire year—no, a lifetime—here reading and never get bored."

Suddenly, as Dumas removed a book from the shelf, he pressed a hidden button and the entire bookshelf revolved, revealing a narrow passageway.

"Voilà, the secret tunnel."

Doug and Lenny glanced at each other, not knowing exactly what to expect.

"Follow me, mes amis," instructed Dumas as he lit a candle in the lantern and led the men down through a long, dark, damp passageway. Doug glanced at his watch, and with a trained instinct reached around to the middle of his back to make sure his M1911 automatic pistol was still there. The lantern projected their long shadows onto the cave walls. It was just wide enough to fit two men walking side by side. Doug and Lenny followed closely behind Dumas.

Lenny remarked, "Wouldn't like to get stuck down here." His voice reverberated off the walls of the passageway. He jumped back as a small mouse scurried by.

As they walked, Dumas told them the tale of the tunnel. His voice echoed slightly off the walls as he began.

"Many centuries ago, the Royals who lived here had an unhappy marriage. The vicious wife was jealous of the young and pretty housekeeper who had caught the eye of her husband. One day, in a fit of temper, the wife threw hot coals from the kitchen fireplace at the housekeeper's eyes, hoping this would make the young maid ugly so her husband would not desire the creature any longer.

The beautiful housekeeper, in her pain and distress, ran from the house as fast as she could. After a few moments, blinded by her tears and the stinging pain from the burning coals, she collapsed and sat crying. The young maid, now blind for life, cried for a very long time and everyplace her tears fell, flowers blossomed on the ground. The husband was so furious he never spoke to his wife again. Although he could not marry the housekeeper because she was considered a commoner, he built a cottage for her on the grounds, surrounded by flowers. He had a tunnel dug that led from his library to the cottage, so when she visited him, she would never have to suffer the winter rain and cold.

The tale has lived on among the villagers, and every time there is a wedding in the village they gather flowers from the garden for the bride and groom to wish them true love and good fortune."

"C'est l'amour," sighed Dumas, wistfully. He continued, "The cottage was later used by the local priest until the entire property was converted to a convent."

Doug noticed the damp and musty smell, and a small alcove off to the left. "What is that alcove?" asked Doug. His mind was racing as he thought this would be the perfect place to smuggle the aristocracy out of France during the revolution—just as they did in the story of *The Scarlet Pimpernel.*

Dumas looked where Doug was pointing.

"I don't know, probably just a place they put their materials or rested when they built the tunnel. There was no significance to that spot that I know of."

Five minutes later, they arrived at what appeared to be the end of the tunnel. Dumas opened up a hidden trapdoor that led inside a small gardener's cottage on the grounds of the chateau. They pulled themselves up through the opening, which appeared to be in the broom closet off to the side of the cottage.

As Doug and Lenny's eyes adjusted to the light, they saw a small, dusty but comfortable room with strong, rugged furniture: an oil lamp on a nightstand next to a single bed in one corner and two wicker rocking chairs by a small stone fireplace. The room was comforting in its simplicity. A small kitchen area to the right, a pantry and a door leading to a bathroom completed the small cottage.

Dumas strolled over to the small kitchen area.

"The local priest used to stay here, but now he lives in the village where he is needed more. He does, however, visit the chateau every morning to say mass. It is with his permission that we have access to the chateau and the cottage. You see, mes amis, he is Polish and his brother is part of our Resistance." Dumas grinned with a wink.

As the men glanced out the wood-shuttered windows on both sides of the fireplace, they saw the chateau in the near distance. Doug guessed it was maybe fifty yards at most. Lenny jabbed Doug lightly in the ribs as he motioned for him to look at what Dumas was doing.

Dumas opened one of the kitchen cabinets, took out some plates and mugs and placed them on the counter. He then proceeded to remove a piece of wood that looked as if it was simply part of the back of the cabinet. To Doug and Lenny's surprise, inside was a complete Morse code transmission setup. Dumas smiled at the men's astonished look as they glanced inside the cabinet and motioned for them to sit in the wicker chairs as he pulled up a stool and began to explain.

"It is from this room that messages reach the Resistance movement by means of a coded broadcast heard on hundreds of clandestine radios." Dumas pulled at his mustache as he resumed talking now more rapidly.

"This is one of our communication setups. From this location we have contact with all resistance groups throughout Europe. I believe you are both familiar with this equipment. I do understand that you have come on behalf of the United States to set up a close relationship with us, and we have checked you out. So let us begin in earnest. The threat from Germany has become imminent," he said most seriously as he lit a cigar. Puffing on it, he continued.

"We have gathered intelligence that Polish prisoners are being rounded up for slaughter, or worse. We are getting some disturbing firsthand stories of experimentation and torture, along with a possible typhoid fever and diphtheria outbreak in one of the prison camps due to contaminated water.

"The SS has invited tenders for a crematorium at Dachau and Buchenwald. We talked previously about the blueprints smuggled out of Germany inside of some thoroughbred horses, compliments of your friend, O'Grady. These are now in the hands of British intelligence. There are rumors of ten thousand Polish prisoners quarantined at an army barrack called Auschwitz, which apparently is conducting atrocious medical experiments." Shaking his head in disgust, he continued.

"As you are aware, Canaris reorganized the Nazi intelligence agency in 1938 into three main sections. The Abwehr section frequently disguises itself by attaching their agents to embassies or trade missions. We here in France are concerned with Klaus Barbie, an SS officer with a line to Himmler. He will do everything in his power to stop our efforts to evacuate innocent people. Barbie has made it one of his top priorities to try to infiltrate our ranks and intercept our communications."

Doug took that as his own cue to begin. "We would like to foster a relationship with the Resistance. In exchange for information and help with establishing safe houses for Americans if the need arises and as a show of good faith, we have brought with us a dose of high-grade penicillin and some medical supplies provided by our government. We can provide more."

Dumas leaned back and crossed his large muscular arms as he nodded in agreement, letting Doug continue.

"The United States is not interested in engaging in war, but we are very concerned with the recent developments overseas," said Doug. "It is in our interest to protect Americans overseas from any escalation in aggression, if such a thing should occur. We are also committed to setting up a joint communications system. We understand that in September, the British received an enigma replica and blueprints which successfully cracked the German codes with your direct help."

Dumas responded proudly as he uncrossed his arms,

"Yes, that is true. Our communications system is good, but we need supplies, medicine, ammunition and weapons. If your country is willing to send us aid, then we will work with you and share with you whatever we know. It must be a mutual relationship of trust."

Doug nodded.

"We want to establish safe houses and passage to the United States for Americans overseas, but also for scientists and physicists trying to escape the Nazi regime who can provide us with technological and scientific advancements. For your help with this, we will provide you with aid." Doug remembered his orders and the authorization given to him in the letter he read in the Secretary's office.

Dumas began to detail what they believed would be occurring within Germany next.

"Through a coded intercept picked up by British intelligence, there is imminent danger of a German attack on Norway and Denmark. We have a communication setup in Copenhagen, compliments of our British counterparts. We know the Germans are highly dependent on the Swedish manufacturing of high-grade iron ore and that the Swedish ports on the Baltic side freeze during the winter."

Dumas continued,

"They are beginning to transport 'heavy water,' the key to a type of reactor in which plutonium can be derived from natural uranium. It is also a source of deuterium oxide which is essential for the production of tritium. This is not a good sign, as our physicist Joliot here in France believes that it may be possible to set up a nuclear chain reaction that most certainly would lead to the construction of a new extremely powerful bomb. The Deuxieme Bureau, which is our military intelligence, removed 185 kg of 'heavy water' from the Vemork plant in Telemark, Norway. It was secretly transported to Scotland and then over here to France."

Doug regarded Dumas intently, his mind ablaze with all he had just heard. Right then he knew with every fiber of his being that there would not only be an invasion, but also another World War. Donovan had been right, and Doug felt he must get this information back to Washington immediately.

"Well, let's see how we can be of assistance to one another. Thank you, Dumas. Our next stop is Copenhagen," said Doug as he and Lenny stood up.

"Excellent," replied Dumas. He smiled and embraced both men in a characteristically European gesture.

"I will give you the contact of a useful person in Denmark. He is British and highly trained in Basque code. By the way, a coder like him that has learned the language in childhood sounds distinctly different from a person who learned the same language in later years. This reduces the possibility of imposters successfully sending false messages. He is also fluent in German, Norwegian, Danish, French and Russian. Do either of you know Basque code?"

Doug was about to answer when Lenny interjected,

"I'm not very familiar with Basque code so I will send in Morse, alright?"

Dumas replied,

"Yes, we can receive from many places. There is no need to tell you all phone lines are monitored, so code your messages whenever you can.

Incidentally, as part of our syndicate, O'Grady has been most helpful to us in smuggling information out of Germany. He has a young boy who has demonstrated an exceptional ability to slip unnoticed into places and listen to conversations for us. Nobody pays much attention to the actions of children. Doug, I understand you have a longstanding relationship with O'Grady based on your common interest in horses?"

Doug nodded affirmatively, thinking about his Basque code instructions in the sealed envelope, but added nothing more to the conversation, silently amazed at the scope of Dumas' information.

Dumas continued as they walked outside the cottage.

"Let's tour the grounds and the chateau now since this will be our primary communication contact point and safe house if needed."

15

Late Night Dr. Spelman's House
Following Day at The Niels Bohr Institute
April 7th

Later that night the shrill ring of the telephone sounded obscenely loud against the quiet of Dr. Spelman's house. His hand shook as he reached to pick up the phone. He knew who it was. He hesitated a moment, considering not picking it up at all. Nevertheless, he knew better. They could be watching him every minute, even when he was at home. Anything was possible with these people. He picked up the receiver. Shaking, Dr. Spelman held it up to his ear and listened.

"I asked you not to call my home line," he barked, trying to sound harsh. He forgot that the housekeeper was not in this week, and there was no one else who would notice if he did not return home. Dr. Spelman lived very much alone and for once, he was deeply regretting it. His wife had left him six months earlier, claiming he was obsessed with his work, and had gone to live with her relatives in Austria.

The dark, combined with his fear, made the house feel claustrophobic. He listened intently to the speaker on the phone, nodding imperceptibly. His shoulders slumped as he realized he must acquiesce to the voice. He hung up and was suddenly very cold. The suffocating silence surrounded him.

♦ ♦ ♦ ♦ ♦ ♦ ♦ ♦ ♦ ♦

The next morning, Dr. Spelman stormed into The Niels Bohr Institute determined to find answers. As he passed through one hallway, Dr. Novak, one of his research colleagues, cornered him.

"Dr. Spelman, good to see you," said Dr. Novak in greeting. "You should have been here yesterday. I could have used your counsel. An experiment of mine has gone terribly wrong…"

Dr. Spelman was distracted and not listening. His patience was beginning to wane. Finally, Dr. Spelman could no longer stand it and abruptly interrupted his colleague.

"Dr. Novak, I must be going. I have important things to attend to. Is Anna in this morning?"

"Why, yes, she is," replied Dr. Novak. "I saw her come in earlier."

With that, Dr. Spelman marched briskly away, leaving a puzzled Dr. Novak in his wake. He was not used to seeing Dr. Spelman so edgy.

Dr. Spelman stormed toward the lab in which Anna was working and threw open the door. Breathing heavily, he glared at her. Anna, startled, looked up from her work.

"Give it to me!" he shouted.

Anna, with her heart pounding furiously, felt the fear and uncertainty rise up in her, although her expression remained calm.

"Give it to me," Dr. Spelman repeated, his eye twitching angrily.

"I want all the notes on the project and the serum!" he demanded.

She breathed a sigh of relief. She knew the notes were useless without the final element, which was tucked safely in the music box under her bed. Anna reached into the drawer of her research desk. She calmly handed Dr. Spelman all her notes. Slowly Anna rose from her desk and walked over to the sealed container. She removed the vial and handed it over to Dr. Spelman.

"I will find the final piece for myself. You should not concern yourself with this project any longer," he stated with hammer-blow finality. "Have you given me everything?"

She nodded slowly as he abruptly turned to leave, slamming the door behind him.

After he left, Anna felt relief wash over her. He did not know yet that she replaced the serum with tap water. Now she no longer had to worry about the final notes themselves, only the microfilm hidden in the ruble and the vial of serum. Her thoughts moved to her sister who had felt so much better this morning. Thus far the serum had worked. Lost in her thoughts, her hand moved absently to the necklace around her neck with the pendant on it, her most treasured possession from her mother.

16

Dr. Spelman's Office at The Niels Bohr Institute
April 7th

Later, in his office, Dr. Spelman frantically searched through the pile of notes and papers for clues, anything to help him solve the formula.

"It must be here," he muttered to himself, his brow wrinkled in concentration. He began to scribble formulas onto a piece of paper. He continued muttering to himself as he crossed out formula after formula that did not work.

I will solve it! He thought, as he continued scribbling.

Suddenly, the door to his office opened. He looked up in annoyance and shouted,

"I thought I told you people to knock!"

His voice trailed off when he saw that it was Lukas and Finn.

Dr. Spelman's previous annoyance melted into fear. Lukas and Finn immediately walked up to his desk. He shrank away, and attempted to hide what he had been doing.

"Your time has run out. You have the money in the account; now we want the final piece of the formula," said Lukas coldly.

"No, no!" yelled Dr. Spelman in a panic.

"You must give me more time! You have the formula. I gave you the remaining serum. There is only one more component to it that I didn't know about. I believe it's possible one of my research scientists has it." Dr. Spelman had not had time to analyze the container of serum and thus did not know it had been replaced with tap water. Likewise Lukas and Finn had not yet delivered the formula to the Kaiser Wilhelm Institute for analysis.

Lukas did not reply; the cords in his throat were bulging. With a look of steel, he threw down pictures of Anna and Britta onto Dr. Spelman's desk. The photos had been taken at various times, indicating that Lukas and Finn must have been following them for some time.

"Just scare them; don't hurt…" Dr. Spelman never finished his plea.

Lukas slammed Spelman's head into the desk, knocking him unconscious. As Dr. Spelman fell onto his desk, Lukas began to gather the papers and Anna's notebook from his desk.

"A deal is a deal," he whispered. "And, we are not finished with you yet. We want the whole thing."

Lukas and Finn arrogantly walked out the door and flicked the light off as they left.

17

Doug and Lenny Arrive in Copenhagen
April 7th

It was a bone-chilling day in April as Doug and Lenny's flight arrived in Copenhagen from Paris where they successfully had made contact and safe-house arrangements through Dumas. As they disembarked the plane, they were greeted with a hearty, "Welcome to Copenhagen," by the flight attendant.

"Enjoy your stay. Please follow me," she said as she smiled at Doug and Lenny, and then proceeded to escort them to the private Ambassadors' Club lounge in the airport. She closed the door, locked it and in one swift movement, quickly removed her medium-length brunette wig, revealing a man.

His voice now much deeper, he bowed with a grand gesture and in a proper British accent said,

"Greetings, gentlemen. I am Alistair Gordon, servant to The United Kingdom, accountant to Her Majesty, The Queen, and counsel to the Bank of England here in Copenhagen." He chuckled as he told them,

"I checked your papers while you were flying over here on the plane."

Noting the flabbergasted look on Lenny and Doug's faces, he continued to remove the makeup and female garments. He laughed, "Surprised?"

No shit, thought Doug.

Alistair looked around the empty room, lowered his voice and with a devilish grin, whispered,

"We British take our theater quite seriously, and the background training at RADA (Royal Academy of Dramatic Arts) in costumes leads to quite good disguises. And, I might add, the Germans fall for a little fräulein every time. Bloody cheeky bastards, I say. My ass is becoming quite sore from being pinched so much." He laughed disarmingly.

"Incidentally, there were two Gestapo operatives on the plane, who are now here in Copenhagen; hence my need for disguise. One of them left his paperwork underneath the dinner tray. So after enough drinks, they did not notice that I removed the trays after their meal, along with the papers that were underneath. Some bloody good information in these papers, lads, confirming some previous Oslo reports on German military plans!"

Lenny and Doug, intrigued, both grinned as they walked to a table in a corner of the empty lounge. As they settled in, Alistair lit a Dunhill cigarette with his gold Dunhill lighter, his long fingers stained yellow.

"The challenge, kind sirs, is in the next performance, as we shall soon see. No doubt our mutual friend, Dumas, has given you a preview." He exhaled tiny, round rings of smoke inside one another and then proceeded to try to poke through them with the cigarette.

Doug and Lenny talked at length with the highly intellectual and charismatic Alistair Gordon, a high-ranking British SOE operative. Alistair's family was the noted 'Gordon's Gin' family and Alistair himself was good friends with Winston Churchill. Alistair had been training at Britain's National Physical Laboratory's Radio Research Station in 1934 when he was asked by Britain's Air Ministry to look into the possibility of transmitting "damaging radiation" as a defense against air attack. Doug and Lenny, who were also trained in radar (acronym for radio detection and ranging) as pilots, were immediately interested.

Alistair continued,

"O'Grady, thanks to his horse dealings, has obtained data on Kraut aircraft production and some plans for aeronautical innovations of prototypes for vertical takeoff and landing of aircraft. I also now have the proposed tanker routes for 'heavy water' headed to Germany, obviously a critical problem." He exhaled, putting out his cigarette in the ashtray and promptly lit another one.

Alistair continued,

"A British invasion of the Faroe Islands, Operation Valentine, is imminent and essential in order to prevent a German invasion. However," he confided again, "the code breakers in London are gathering increased chatter and information that the Luftwaffe is talking about an Operation Weserübung. There is no news yet on what that is, although the reports about the gathering of the German fleet in Danish waters were received on April 4th. I have been informed by London headquarters that your commanding officer has assigned you both to this mission.

"The Danish fleet has been ordered not to engage, and incidentally, they only have two infantry divisions in Zealand and Jutland. The British Navy and the French are planning to mine the inland waters of Norway and force German shipping out into the Atlantic where the Royal Navy can better intercept the German ships."

Lenny and Doug gathered from their conversation with Alistair that Dumas was also involved in this, given that he had already shared some of this information with them in Paris. As they were walking out of the lounge, Doug asked Alistair to relay a message to Dumas saying they would return to Paris before they went back to the US. The men stood up and shook hands as Alistair said,

"We'll be in touch."

Both men were tired and looked slightly dazed as the time change started to catch up with them. Alistair Gordon was indeed a wealth of knowledge, as well as a man of contradiction, and all this information needed to be encoded and sent back to Washington as soon as possible. As Doug and Lenny stepped out of the Ambassadors' Club into the main terminal at the Copenhagen Airport, Alistair did not. The men hailed a taxi in the gloomy rain.

"Alistair's appearance, with that disguise and comical manner, is remarkably deceptive, don't you think?" Doug remarked to Lenny. "I'll bet people underestimate him all the time, and it serves him well. That is one very smart man. MI6 is lucky to have him."

"True, he's quite a character! Good thing I didn't try to pinch his ass on the plane." Lenny chuckled in amusement.

Doug nodded absently, his mind churning as he stared off into the distance.

"I'm exhausted," exclaimed Lenny as he climbed into the taxi.

"I think I'm going to check into the hotel and work on getting myself together again with a good scotch and some shuteye."

Doug was about to climb into the taxi with Lenny when his hand brushed the mysterious letter crumpled in his breast pocket.

"I almost forgot. I have a family friend to meet while we're here. I think I will go visit him now while we have a little downtime," he told Lenny.

"We don't know where this mission will take us or how fast, so I may not get another chance. We can meet back at the hotel in a few hours. I'll get the next taxi. You go on ahead."

Lenny looked mildly surprised but nodded without questioning Doug further. Doug moved off to find his own taxi, all thoughts trained on the unknown man he was about to visit.

18

God Bless the Child that Got His Own
April 7th

In the taxi, Doug gazed out on the bustling streets of downtown Copenhagen filled with busy people shopping, laughing, biking and otherwise going about their business. The downpour had stopped, and the streets were bright and clean. He felt a twinge of envy. There were times when he wished he could be a part of the normal populace. He sighed, "I am doing this for my country." His corporate career would have to remain on hold for now.

As time passed, the streets became less crowded and the city gave way to the countryside. He began to doze when suddenly he felt the cab pull to a stop. They were in front of a charming chalet surrounded by a white picket fence and a flagstone walkway leading up to the front door. Behind the cottage was a large barn, presumably used as a garage and for storage. Doug's mind was instantly alert; he breathed in deeply and glanced at his watch—it was showtime and he was curious. Handing the driver his fare, he got out of the taxi and stepped into the cool spring air.

Good thing I brought a warm jacket, he thought, shivering for a moment. He stood on the sidewalk in front of the house before proceeding up the walkway. Just then, a stunning young blonde with fabulous legs and another younger, sickly-looking woman opened the door and left Cunningham's cottage. They smiled a pleasant "hello" before hurrying to flag his taxi. He couldn't help but notice the blonde's vibrant violet eyes. His senses were immediately on high alert. He watched her until they got in the cab.

I wonder…who he is, and why those two gals are leaving his house in the middle of the day. He averted his thoughts from the blonde and moved towards the cottage cautiously. Arriving at the door, he hesitated and reached around to his back to make sure his custom-made Smith & Wesson pistol was still there. "Just a precautionary measure," he told himself, knowing he was showing up unannounced.

Before he could raise his hand to knock, the door swung open and Doug was suddenly face-to-face with an athletically fit, handsome man in his eighties. He had a full head of wavy gray hair and bright green eyes, the mirror image of Doug's own eyes. He was leaning ever so slightly, on a walking cane, and wore gray slacks and a cashmere blue sweater. He smiled, though his eyes betrayed a deep and lasting sadness.

Extending his hand, a pleasant, calm, deep baritone voice said,

"You must be Douglas. I am Johann Cunningham. This is indeed a pleasure." He noticed how much Doug's smile reminded him of Doug's mother's smile while ushering him into the house.

Doug noticed he called him by his full name. Only his mother had ever called him Douglas. *How strange…and how did he know I was coming to visit?*

"I see you passed Anna and Britta on your way in. Lovely girls," Dr. Cunningham murmured, feeling a need to explain their presence due to the curious look in Doug's eyes.

Very good, noticed an astute Dr. Cunningham, *they trained him well. Good! I must remember to thank Donovan personally*, as he noticed Doug quickly scanning his surroundings.

He continued,

"Anna was one of my pupils, something akin to an exchange student, at Oxford University. She started there at age sixteen. I taught part-time while practicing medicine there and in Germany. Anna is quite the research scientist at The Niels Bohr Institute—she and her sister lived in my cottage in Oxford with my Aunt Mary and Gretel, my housekeeper. They are like surrogate daughters to me. I was hoping to introduce you, but Anna had to get her sister, Britta, back home as, unfortunately, Britta has been quite ill. Anna came by to get my opinion on a matter concerning her research.

"But do come in. May I take your coat? I apologize for rambling on, it happens with age," said Dr. Cunningham with an endearing smile, as Doug handed him his jacket.

"Please, let's have a seat in the kitchen. I have a warm fire going, and I will start some coffee. It's a bit warmer in there." He indicated the way to the kitchen with his cane.

As Doug moved through the sitting room to the kitchen, his trained eyes took in every detail of the room. The inside was small and he noticed that a few Dutch oil paintings—very good ones—decorated the walls. On the mahogany desk in the corner, there was an old notebook lying open, and he noticed a drawing of a pentacle on one page alongside a display of antique fountain pens. There were some porcelain figures, a small framed picture of a hand-crocheted pentacle, and some small framed photographs. It also looked like Dr. Cunningham had taken apart a radio set as there were pieces scattered on the desk as well. The book-lined walls containing mostly medical texts and some pieces of well-carved furniture gave the room a masculine, lived-in presence.

"Can I offer you something? Tea, Danish coffee or something stronger, perhaps?" asked the older man, catching Doug's look at his desk. He added, "Don't mind the mess. I am always tinkering with some device or another."

"I'm fine, thank you. Please don't trouble yourself. I am curious about your letter, though. You mentioned my mother," replied Doug getting right to the point as he looked around, noticing again the old framed pictures on the desk in the corner. One resembled the picture of his mother that he carried in his wallet. He noticed a small black fly next to it and his immediate reaction was to shoo it away or kill it, but out of politeness, Doug said nothing. *Why would Dr. Cunningham have that photo? I'm sure that's a picture of my mother* he thought while he followed Dr. Cunningham into the kitchen.

Dr.Cunningham walked slowly into the kitchen and turned off the radio on the counter. He sat at the square kitchen table while Doug chose a chair opposite him. Both men looked at each other. Their resemblance to one another was striking, like looking into a mirror.

"You must be wondering why I asked you to come all this way to visit with me?" Dr. Cunningham began slowly.

Doug nodded, noting Dr. Cunningham's now serious demeanor.

"What I am about to tell you was not something I could write in a letter or say over the phone, as it is quite personal. As you are very well aware, communication these days is not safe and we believe most of the phone lines are compromised."

Doug looked at him, waiting for him to continue. He knew instinctively that this meeting would dramatically change his life. He never imagined how this could involve his mother, but the picture in the sitting room had alarmed him. Something here was amiss.

"It's all right," Doug replied amicably, wanting to put the older man at ease so he could find out why their meeting was so urgent.

"I always wanted to see Copenhagen and now, as luck would have it, I am here on business for forty-eight hours."

"If I may, let me start at the beginning of my story then," said Dr. Cunningham. "My friends call me Johann, although I am mostly Scottish, hence the last name Cunningham. It originates from the Cunningham area in the Ayrshire district of Scotland.

"One of my grandmothers was a feisty Dane; she was my favorite. This home that I live in now was once hers. I studied medicine at Oxford University, and then continued on to practice at one of the German University hospitals with a specialty in neurology. I studied infectious diseases that present themselves at the brain and central nervous system. After some time in Berlin, I was offered a position at Oxford to conduct research on a breakthrough drug called penicillin, still in its infancy. I now live most of the year here, still returning to London quite often and the short golf vacations in the south of Spain when it gets too cold." Dr. Cunningham smiled and continued,

"I met your mother while she was visiting Europe on a writing assignment for an American newspaper during the Great War. The paper just happened to be owned by your grandfather."

Doug nodded, adding to the conversation,

"I remember my grandfather always seemed bigger than life," he smiled, genuinely trying to lighten up the conversation. His grandfather had been a very controlling man and he did not want to get into that conversation.

Just where is Cunningham going with this? Doug curiously looked over at the older man.

Cunningham took a sip of water and put his glass back down on the table. He slowly got up from the table and walked with the help of his cane towards the stove.

"I think I will make some coffee." He hesitated a moment and turned to look at Doug. His green eyes looked steadily at Doug's eyes.

"Your mother's husband was an American officer whose entire Army regiment was presumed dead from mustard gas poisoning. They had been reported missing for over six months."

Doug began to consider this, as brief and fleeting memories filled his head.

"It was many years ago, long before you were born. I remember," continued Dr. Cunningham, his voice now lower and filled with emotion, "how beautiful and sweet your mother was. Douglas, I cannot begin to tell you how utterly and totally consumed with grief I was to hear of her death."

Dr. Cunningham's voice wavered slightly, but he went on.

"Douglas, I tried in vain to reach her for years, but my letters were returned. I met your mother because she had requested an interview with me. I had written a publication on the effects of chemical warfare on the central nervous system. I believe she was trying to come to grips with her grief over her husband. Distraught, she confided in me that she had been suffering from severe headaches, which I believed were stress induced, due to the loss of her husband."

Dr. Cunningham looked at the floor, hesitated, then looked up at Doug and quietly said,

"Douglas, I'm not sure how to tell you this, but we fell in love. I knew, without question, that I would never love another woman as I did your mother. I never married."

Douglas shifted uncomfortably in his chair, but said nothing as Dr. Cunningham continued.

"I wanted to marry her, but a telegram from your grandfather was delivered to her in Germany stating that her husband was alive but gravely wounded. He was in a hospital in Virginia. She had to go back to the United States immediately. Her passage on one of the ships had already been booked for her by your grandfather. I selfishly hoped she would change her mind and stay with me.

"Two years ago, I received a letter forwarded to me from one of my neighbors in Germany. It appears that my next-door neighbors' relatives found it in their deceased aunt's mail years later. A stupid mistake on the part of the postal system that changed all of our lives. Kindly, the neighbors sent it to Oxford, and then it was forwarded here.

"My pride and bitterness prevented me from opening it. I did not open the letter until a few months ago. She had passed away so many years ago and I never knew; we don't always get US papers here. You must have been a young boy at the time.

"I also learned that her husband passed away shortly after her return to the United States. A friend of mine visiting the US a few months ago looked her up in the Virginia newspaper archives and informed me of her death. It was then that I opened the letter which had stayed in my desk all these years."

Dr. Cunningham walked into the sitting room, opened his desk drawer and removed a yellowed letter from an envelope along with a photograph; he handed them both to Doug.

Doug looked at the photo of himself as a young boy holding his mother's hand. He began to read to himself. Intense emotions swelled up in his throat, and for the first time since his mother's death, he struggled to keep his emotions in check. He slowly read the letter in which his mother told Dr. Cunningham she had learned she was pregnant upon arriving in the United States.

Dr. Cunningham looked at him and said softly,

"Douglas, you are my son, my only child. If only I had known."

Both men sat there in silence. A tear rolled down Dr. Cunningham's face; he quickly wiped it away. Doug continued to stare at him blankly.

How can this be true? Doug's memories flowed spontaneously, the cause and effect sequences becoming crystal clear. "You, my father, my mother…" began Douglas, struggling for words. And then everything began to click—the file processing in his head and the churning in his gut—it all added up. He was trained to be in control, so he regrouped his emotions to speak. "My mother once mentioned a friend from Germany; a doctor, now that I recall, but I was never told any of this."

Dr. Cunningham nodded and took a sip from the glass of water beside him. Doug began to lose his composure, struggling again to find the right words. He thought of the picture in his wallet that he had always put on his instrument panel for good luck when he was flying. He looked up.

Finally, Doug said,

"This is quite a surprise. Why are you telling me now?"

Dr. Cunningham did not respond immediately. "I thought about coming to the United States to tell you myself, but I'm getting on in years. I did not know how you might react."

Doug pushed his chair away from the table to leave.

"I appreciate you telling me this. Incidentally, are those pictures of my mother?" asked Doug, as he motioned to the sitting room.

"Yes, you are welcome to them, Douglas."

The older man's face clouded, as his smile was replaced with a fleeting look of anguish, as he regarded his son. He had not expected this to be easy, and he knew it might take Doug some time to process this information.

"Douglas," he began again, "before you leave, I want you to know that I am so sorry I can't make up for those lost years. My only consolation is that someday I will sail to that far distant shore and be with the love of my life again."

"I appreciate your honesty, only it's a little late. I grew up without a dad, my mother died of a brain aneurysm, I went to boarding school, then to MIT and subsequently excelled in aviation. I have a good life, and you are not part of it. I thank you for sharing this with me. I know it could not have been an easy decision for you—whether or not to tell me that you are my father. I just wish…"

Doug was now visibly agitated. He got up and started towards the front door, seeking to get outside and clear the thoughts swirling in his head. He noticed the fly again on the desk in the same position. Dr. Cunningham followed behind.

"Thank you for coming, Douglas. I know this is difficult," said Dr. Cunningham. Doug turned and looked into Dr. Cunningham's eyes, so like his own, shook his hand and left the cottage with the letter and the photo of him and his mother.

Once settled in a cab headed back to the city, Doug felt angry and conflicted. Despite not wanting to, he liked the man. Cunningham's candor and honesty had struck him right in the heart. He wondered how much suffering these two star-crossed lovers had gone through. What a twist of fate. Both of his parents had lived alone for so many years never knowing what happiness they could have shared.

Through this bizarre set of circumstances, he had grown up without a father. Then at a young age, he had lost his mother. He wondered how difficult it was for his mother who believed, after her husband died, that the one man she truly loved—the father of her son—would not answer her letters. Still, knowing his mother's integrity, he knew she would have stood by the man she married until he passed away. After he died, however, she had been free to be with her true love, except that the postal system had gone astray. How ironic.

All he wanted right now was a stiff scotch and a good night's sleep.

Damn it! All of my military training did not prepare me for this crap.

♦ ♦ ♦ ♦ ♦ ♦ ♦ ♦ ♦ ♦

19

Copenhagen Hotel
April 7th

Slowly coming out of his reverie, Doug realized the cab was back in the hustle and bustle of the city as the taxi passed the statue of *The Little Mermaid*. He suddenly felt lost and lonely. He stared out of the window, feeling like a lost soul in need of rescue from this emotional overload.

He changed mental gears and directed his thoughts to his counter espionage or CE mission as he had been taught. CE—although the term was often misunderstood—was an offensive operation, a means of obtaining intelligence about an operation by attempting to use the opposition's operations. Its purpose was not to apprehend enemy agents. Doug knew that the goal of all CE operations was to penetrate the opposition's own secret operations' apparatus. The Germans knew this as well.

If you shared your opponent's mind and thinking to a reliable degree, you knew what he knew, thereby annulling in one stroke the value of his secret intelligence about you. As Doug continued thinking about this, he realized he would be working with some of the best. Alistair and Dumas were highly trained.

Doug thought about how O'Grady and Alistair had been successful with the Abwehr. As Doug stretched his legs in the back of the taxi, he thought again about bits of his conversation with Dumas, Alistair and O'Grady. His instincts were telling him that something was going to happen very soon in Denmark. He knew the Danes and the Norwegians did not have the forces to defend themselves, and consequently, they would be up for grabs between the Germans and the British.

How many people, he pondered as the taxi passed by the Royal Palace of the oldest monarchy in Europe, *will die because of this war*. This was more of a rhetorical statement than a question. *Perhaps history just keeps on repeating itself, and man will never learn. It is not within the capability of the beast*, he thought ironically, as his mind drifted back to his mother and Dr. Cunningham, his father.

I now have a father; but what good is discovering a father at my age? I'll deal with that later. He felt unsettled and weary.

As the cab slowed its approach upon reaching the front of the hotel, the colorful evening twilight started to unfold.

The taxi stopped in front of a restored granary from the 1780s. It had since become a luxury hotel with the Royal Palace on its starboard side and central Copenhagen on its portside. Located on the corner was the ornate main branch of the Bank of Denmark. The hotel's rustic charm, raw brick walls and two hundred-year-old joists of Pomeranian pine, complete with a sauna and bar, made it a perfect destination for businessmen traveling to Copenhagen.

Doug entered the hotel lobby and stopped at the bar for a scotch. A freshly showered Lenny greeted him, dressed and anxiously waiting to get started on a night out on the town.

"Good nap, then?" commented Doug.

"We're goin' out, remember?" quipped Lenny as he took in Doug's tired face.

"We are, huh?" replied Doug, groaning. He was mentally weary from his shocking news and physically exhausted from jet lag. He did not feel at all like going out. All he wanted was a scotch, a hot shower and sleep.

"Yeah, it will be fun and we need some good amusement. I hear Louis Armstrong is playing this club tonight. I heard him in New York a few years ago and he is great," said Lenny enthusiastically, "so go get ready!"

"I'm ready as is," smiled Doug, who was an enthusiastic jazz lover and an accomplished pianist in his own right.

"Really? I thought the idea was to appeal to the ladies, not frighten them." Lenny gave him a look that suggested he looked truly terrible.

"Whatever you say, partner. Give me some time to shower and change my clothes," said Doug, giving in.

Lenny replied with a grin, "All right. Go get ready!"

"Listen, Lenny, better yet, I'll meet you in the lobby in two hours. I desperately need some rest, and we need to get Alistair and Dumas' info transmitted back to Washington." Doug looked at his watch.

"Okay. I suppose I can amuse myself for a while. Take your time." Glancing again at Doug, he really did look exhausted.

◆ ◆ ◆ ◆ ◆ ◆ ◆ ◆ ◆ ◆

Outside a Copenhagen strip club in a back alleyway, women were screaming. One of them had just found the decapitated body of one of the strippers when they had stepped outside the back door for a quick smoke.

A lone figure kept walking, his sexual urge now satisfied, the echo of screams pleasing to his ears.

◆ ◆ ◆ ◆ ◆ ◆ ◆ ◆ ◆ ◆

Later that evening, Lenny and Doug departed to enjoy the sparkling nightlife of Copenhagen. As they left the hotel, Lenny looked excited; Doug still looked exhausted.

◆ ◆ ◆ ◆ ◆ ◆ ◆ ◆ ◆ ◆

20

Early Evening in Copenhagen
April 7th

Anna, having just stepped out of a steaming bubble bath, stood in front of her bathroom mirror wrapped in a white towel, brushing her hair. Today was Britta's twenty-first birthday. She was glad she could celebrate this day with her sister. There had been so many of Britta's birthdays when either Anna had had to work or Britta had been too weak to lift her head from the pillow, much less go dancing.

Thank God she's alive, and not only that, but also doing so well. The serum worked, she thought. She did not notice the two men below in the shadows on the street corner looking up at the steamed window. Anna began dreamily brushing her hair a hundred strokes to make it shine. Her white silk sheath dress was laid out, ready on her bed. Tonight she had plans to have a great time and forget about work. It had been a long time since she had let go and had fun.

Her thoughts wandered back to her days at Oxford and her various dates. Most of the men bored her, and it was always the same questions: Where were you born? What does your father do? Invariably, once some of the Oxford students learned she was of the Russian working class they found her unacceptable to bring home to their families. Then there were the others whose sole motivation was to get her into bed.

Someday I will find my soul mate, thought Anna as she stood up and gently slipped the dress over her head.

Dr. Spelman was starting to get on her nerves. He was exerting constant pressure about the formula, but his attentions had also become personal. *Just last week he pinned me against the filing cabinet with his whole body for a few moments and then pretended it was an accident,* thought Anna. She hadn't had to deal with that kind of behavior since her first week at the Institute when Dr. Spelman had tried to steal a kiss. After she said no, there had been no further problems. *What happened to change him?* she wondered uneasily.

It will not be long before he realizes I have replaced the remaining serum in the lab with tap water, she thought, knowing that it was only a matter of time before she lost her position.

"Anna, let's go!" cried her sister excitedly from the next room.

"I'll be ready shortly," Anna called back as she applied her lipstick. No sooner were the words out of her mouth when her sister entered the bathroom in a gorgeous red halter dress, giggling. Anna gazed at her sister in the mirror.

The change in her is absolutely amazing, she thought. Britta's face was fuller and there were no longer dark circles under her eyes. Her skin was flushed with a vivid pink hue instead of the usual jaundiced yellow.

"You look beautiful," complimented Anna. Her sister smiled.

"Well, we need to get going," replied Britta, "or we'll miss the night." Her eyes twinkled mischievously. Anna nodded.

Anna looked luminous. She was wearing a lovely white dress that draped over one shoulder that made her look like a statuesque Greek goddess. It complemented her golden skin tone and brought out the sparkle in her violet eyes. Her hair fell in waves below her shoulders tonight. She looked at herself in the mirror.

This will have to do. She straightened out a silk stocking by refastening it to her garter. Once downstairs, she grabbed her coat and noticed a torn piece of paper between the cushions on the sitting room couch. *I'll have to get that later,* as she ran up the stairs, to her bedroom and removed her pendant. She took the shoebox from the floorboard under the bed, removed the ruble with the gold chain from the music box, pried it open and placed the pendant inside. She then clasped the gold chain around her neck and put the music box back into its hiding place.

"Anna, hurry up!" cried an impatient Britta who was waiting by the front door with keys in hand.

♦ ♦ ♦ ♦ ♦ ♦ ♦ ♦ ♦ ♦

Anna and Britta left their townhouse, taking no notice of the two predatory men watching them from the opposite end of the street. Oblivious to the men, Britta and Anna laughed and skipped merrily down the street into the nightlife of Copenhagen.

Lukas took a long drag of his cigarette then stamped it out on the ground. The two men followed the girls, being careful not to walk too closely behind.

♦ ♦ ♦ ♦ ♦ ♦ ♦ ♦ ♦ ♦

All around the city, neon lights and exhilarating music filled the crowded streets. Free-spirited people spilled from the doorways as Britta and Anna approached the energetic dinner-dance-jazz club called The Lantern. A long line had formed inside a red velvet roped area that was reserved for VIP guests.

The bald, Russian club owner, seeing Britta, waved them through the crowd. As they made their way to him, a few people waiting in line called out to Britta, recognizing her from the times she had performed there in the past. Anna recognized Viktor from the few times she had stopped in to watch Britta sing, but that had been months ago before Britta's health had started to deteriorate rapidly. Anna felt a twinge of guilt, as many nights she had been asleep before Britta got home in the wee hours after her performance. She shrugged it off, knowing that her job at the Institute demanded early mornings and long hours.

"Britta you look stunning," Viktor said smiling, as he enthusiastically greeted her, planting a kiss right on her lips. He then proceeded to kiss Anna's hand. Anna laughed, somewhat startled by his seeming familiarity with Britta. He led them to a reserved white linen table, and snapped his fingers for the waiter and shouted,

"Bring a bottle of Dom Perignon Champagne, only the best for the birthday girl" as he pulled out the chair for her.

"Thank you Viktor. You are so sweet." Britta charmingly smiled at him as she took her seat.

Viktor replied,

"I am delighted that you have brought your beautiful sister, this evening. I am honored by your presence, Madame. Now if you two will excuse me for a few moments, I must attend to our guest, Mr. Armstrong. Britta, I hope we shall see you sing at intermission darling." The girls looked at each other and giggled as he left.

♦ ♦ ♦ ♦ ♦ ♦ ♦ ♦ ♦ ♦

Lukas and Finn entered the club shortly afterwards without incident and made a straight line for the girls' table. They were big, powerfully built men whose muscles rippled and bulged visibly beneath the confines of their shirts. They started aggressively to harass Anna and Britta to dance.

♦ ♦ ♦ ♦ ♦ ♦ ♦ ♦ ♦ ♦

21

Jazz Club in Copenhagen
April 7th

Doug and Lenny entered the smoky, dark jazz club, The Lantern. Doug nonchalantly scanned the dimly lit club. As they took a seat at the bar, Lenny flagged the bartender and ordered their drinks. Doug, still scanning the room, immediately noticed the blonde woman and recognized her instantly from Dr. Cunningham's cottage. She sat at a far corner table with a younger, dark-haired woman. He knew instinctively it had to be "Anna" with the ailing sister of whom Cunningham had spoken. However, the sister did not look very sick tonight. In fact, she was striking.

Witnessing the two muscled men harassing the girls, who were visibly upset, he turned to Lenny.

"Lenny, check out the blonde guy's neck over there." Both men turned and looked toward the girls' table. Even under the dim club lights, they could see the swastika on his neck.

"Doug, those guys might be Gestapo. We shouldn't interfere. Remember, we are supposed to be neutral and civilians."

Doug shook his head in disagreement. "Lenny, we have to. Those women at that table are friends of the man I met with today. They were at his house and, as it turns out, he is a family member. It looks as if those idiots are giving them a hard time."

"Okay, buddy," Lenny agreed after eyeballing the situation again. "Let's show them some Yankee style." Lenny and Doug walked over to where the girls were sitting.

"Gentlemen, you need to show some respect to the fairer sex," said Doug in a low, threatening voice to the swastika'd blonde fellow, who turned and scowled. Growling, he threw a punch at Doug who quickly dodged it. Doug caught him by the wrist and in a swift martial arts move landed him on the floor.

A feisty brawl broke out. The four men were well matched as all were highly trained fighters. Both Lenny and Doug were carrying their pistols but were reluctant to use them. Suddenly one of the men dug in his pocket and, with the flip of his wrist, snapped open a switchblade. He aimed the glinting switchblade at Doug's throat. The fight reeled outside onto the sidewalk in front of the club with onlookers cheering for Doug and Lenny. Just then a high-ranking German officer pulled up in a chauffeur-driven car. The crowd moved aside.

"What are you doing?" he demanded in a loud, authoritative shout. He directed his question at the two Germans who stood at attention immediately.

"I will report you—these are Americans, and as such, they are neutral in the Führer's eyes. Are you trying to start a war with America?" he asked in German.

Lukas and Finn reluctantly left, disgruntled and badly bloodied. The crowd moved back inside. The German officer pulled Doug and Lenny towards the back alley, then removed his hat and moustache.

"You bloody Yanks, what are you doing mixing it up with the Gestapo? You're really going to get their knickers in a twist, bloody nerve they've got coming in here," said the man, his British voice brimming with comical undertones.

Doug and Lenny realized it was Alistair Gordon, the master of disguises, and laughed with relief as they tried to catch their breath.

"I'll meet you inside the club after I change, and don't get into any more trouble. We've got our hands full as it is; there are rumors that an invasion is imminent."

Doug and Lenny returned to the club and both ordered shots of vodka. Doug looked at Lenny and raised his glass.

"Sköl," he said, "when in Rome…" and he drained the shot and put it down on the bar for another. The club owner was nowhere in sight.

♦ ♦ ♦ ♦ ♦ ♦ ♦ ♦ ♦ ♦

One look from a woman's eye makes you the happiest man in the world."

22

Dinner Dance at the Jazz Club
Later that Evening—April 7th

Anna had been watching the fight all along and now walked up to Doug and Lenny who were sitting at the bar.

"Thank you," she said to both of them, blushing a little in spite of herself.

Doug and Lenny, both grinning, responded in unison,

"You are most welcome."

Anna looked at Doug curiously at first and noticed his green eyes that seemed to see right through to her soul. They looked very familiar, although she knew she had never met him before. "Weren't you at Dr. Cunningham's house earlier today?" she asked, her violet eyes sparkling as she looked directly at him.

I could get lost in those eyes, thought Doug. He felt an overwhelming magnetic attraction to her so strong it made his senses reel. Anna recognized his accent to be American when he introduced himself and Lenny. He told her he was a businessman from Virginia.

"What brings you to Copenhagen?" asked Anna innocently, looking up at him through her lush, black eyelashes.

Doug looked discreetly at Anna's graceful silhouette with an appreciative glance down her endlessly long legs. His charming, crooked smile served only to bring attention to his

111

strong jaw line and perfect white teeth. "Apparently, I'm here to save you," he chuckled.

His deep voice resonated down to her toes. She smiled, and blushed again, enamored by his silliness as she dipped her handkerchief in a glass of water and proceeded to dab the cuts on Doug's knuckles and forehead.

Doug's adrenaline kicked into higher gear. Plus, he felt rather chivalrous after the fight and empowered by her presence. In fact, there was an inexplicable emotion taking over, one he had never felt before.

Anna smiled at Doug and asked, "Why don't you both join me and my sister at our table? It is the least I can do for saving us from those horrid men. We are celebrating her twenty-first birthday!" Both men were more than happy to oblige.

Anna and Doug, mesmerized by each other, were both silent at the table, waiting for the other to speak. Doug thought of a quote from somewhere, *There is something here greater than what meaningless words can utter; it is not the syllables uttered from our lips and mouths that bring our hearts together, but a silence that illuminates my soul by just being around her.* The attraction was overwhelming. Neither of them had ever felt this kind of instant, powerful, magnetic sexual energy before.

Britta did much of the talking at first with Lenny. She was vivacious and happy in a way Anna had seldom seen. Anna was shy for the moment, and Doug, normally glib with women, was equally tongue-tied. Doug and Anna just looked at each other, equally surprised by their mutual attraction. Finally, Anna spoke and began telling Doug about her studies and career as a research scientist at Oxford and The Niels Bohr Institute.

As the waitress brought over their dinners, Doug told entertaining stories about growing up in Virginia, going to boarding school and playing football with Lenny, enjoying the laughter of both girls and the ambiance of the club. As Anna and Doug talked with one another, Lenny and Britta did the same.

Lenny motioned to Doug.

"I'm going to take this beautiful birthday girl to the dance floor. Care to join?"

Doug looked at him.

"Maybe in a moment, you two have fun. We'll join you shortly."

Britta was enjoying herself and moved onto the floor for a dance with Lenny, leaving Anna and Doug alone at the table.

"Last week, Britta did not have enough strength to walk much less laugh, talk and dance with a handsome man. I am amazed she is so much better now."

Doug asked, "Are you married?" suddenly feeling awkward at the spontaneity of his question.

Surprised at his blunt question, Anna laughed.

"Yes, to my work. Up until now, I have spent most of my life inside a research lab and somehow the other scientists never interested me romantically. How about you?"

Doug grinned.

"Never got close enough. Perhaps because I lost my mother at a young age." Doug waved the cocktail waitress over and ordered more champagne.

"Oh Doug, I am so sorry. How old were you? What happened? I'm sorry, am I being too personal?"

"No, that's fine. I was eight and we were living in Virginia. I remember my mother was hanging linens in the backyard and a storm started blowing in. I stopped playing to run to my mother, but she had already collapsed on the ground. I believe she had a brain aneurysm. I thought my father was a World War I veteran which is why I became interested in aviation." Doug was still cautious to share more information.

"I'm sorry, Doug. I do understand what it's like. My mother also died when I was young, but at least I still had my father and Britta. She is not only my younger sister, but also my best friend."

After the waitress delivered the champagne, they resumed their conversation as if there were no one else in the club.

"What a coincidence that we saw each other at Dr. Cunningham's this morning. He told me that he is my father. I just learned that today from a letter my mother had written to him many years ago." He ground out the last sentence, still confused and angry about the news. He wasn't sure why he had just decided to share this information with her. He suddenly wondered if he should have just kept it to himself.

Anna picked up on the anger and dismay that flitted across Doug's face in the quickest of seconds and responded kindly, "Doug, I can understand how that news must be quite a shock to you. If it's any reassurance, I have known Dr. Cunningham since my days at Oxford and he is not only brilliant, but he is also…to quote—'A man whose wealth has made him kind and whose kindness has made him wealthy."

Anna went on.

"It is, however, strange we should meet at this juncture. I do believe the universe moves to its own rhythm, so perhaps this is fate—kismet. There are no accidents."

She smiled charmingly as she continued,

"I looked to him as a father figure and you actually have him now as a papa. Should I be jealous?" she asked with a teasing smile.

"I haven't really digested all of it yet," admitted Doug, wrinkling his forehead as if trying to solve the mysteries of human existence much less his own life.

Anna continued,

"He worked with one of my professors on crystallogy and is one of the pioneers in the development of high-grade penicillin, which will cure many infections if they can ever figure out how to make it in large quantities."

Anna smiled, feeling she had known Doug all her life. She felt this intuitively, not in a way that was easily quantifiable or explainable. Its knowledge was directly stored in her unconscious' database, and she knew right then she could, and would, trust him with her life.

"Doug, if you have inherited any of his genetic makeup, you are a lucky man."

"Anna, you really do think and talk naturally in scientific lingo, don't you?" Doug teased. He asked more about the scientific research she did, and she elaborated as much as she could without going into "boring" detail. Doug felt he could listen to her read the dictionary and not be bored. He was also intrigued by her level of knowledge.

Anna asked,

"What are your thoughts? Do you think we are on the brink of war? Is Copenhagen in danger?"

Doug replied philosophically,

"Well, it seems inevitable. Man is greedy by nature. Anna, I don't know what will happen, but I urge you to be extremely careful. The Nazi party seems to be very interested in acquiring scientists and their research."

Anna considered Dr. Spelman's recent odd behavior, but dismissed it for now. She would talk to Doug about that later.

Anna revealed Britta's recovery to Doug. "I am especially protective of Britta because she had become increasingly sick over the years. And as of a few days ago, she was on the verge of dying. But now, miraculously, she is okay."

"How is such a miracle possible?"

Anna was reluctant to respond at first. But she intuitively trusted Doug in a way she had never trusted anyone. She told him,

"In my research, I found a way to make her better based on my mother's healing notebook and my own childhood observations of natural, unexplainable healings in Russia. It has to do with restoring cellular structure that is damaged. I found the missing link on protein strands that came from a hot sulphur spring near our village. My belief is that it can restore a damaged cell. However, there is still much testing that needs to be done as it could be very dangerous." That was all she decided to say for the moment.

Doug was intrigued by the revelation.

"Our president, Franklin Delano Roosevelt, afflicted with polio, has been advised by his doctors to sit in the hot sulphur water springs in Saratoga, New York, and Greenbrier, West Virginia, among other places, to ease his pain."

Anna told him,

"The sulphur springs back home healed Britta's cut when she was a child, even though she had been diagnosed as a hemophiliac, a rare disease for a girl; it is usually passed down to a male child from the mother. This formula has the possibility to repair the damaged membrane around a cell, thus making it a possible cure for damaged cells and possibly other diseases."

"It sounds like you may have saved her life, Anna, if indeed it is this formula that worked. You took quite a chance giving it to her. This is an amazing discovery. What will you do with it?" he inquired.

Anna, still cautious, replied,

"It is a work that still needs much research, plus there is very little of it left. The only reason I dared to try it on Britta was because she was dying, so there was nothing to lose and no time to spare," Anna shuddered. "It could have gone so wrong. I also got very lucky it worked!"

Doug shook his head,

"Yes, I understand. But why can't you go back to the sulphur spring and get more?"

Anna replied,

"We went back, but an earthquake had devastated the entire village. My father was one of the casualties. I looked everywhere for the spring but it was no longer there, no doubt swallowed back up by the earth. Even our house was destroyed."

They looked over at the bar to see that Lenny and Britta were enjoying watching Louis Armstrong onstage.

Doug took Anna's hand and pulled her up to dance as Louis Armstrong sang,

"Give me a kiss to build a dream on…" Doug closed his eyes and traced his fingers down Anna's spine as their bodies moved perfectly together; she felt the hardness of his lean muscular body pressing against hers. He kissed her lips; her mouth was soft and full of heat and promise.

Anna's pulse tripled as her belly filled with butterflies. This was a man who knew exactly how she wanted to be kissed. This was the man she would choose to spend the rest of her life, if only they could manage to survive the current world turmoil.

At the show's intermission, the crowd implored Britta to sing. She had sang there occasionally on her good days and had become quite a favorite. Doug offered to play the piano and accompany her.

The owner of the club, Viktor, walked up to the group, took Britta's hand and kissed it.

"Britta, I would be honored if you would sing for us." With Lenny's insistence, Britta shyly got onstage and sang a beautiful rendition of a popular blues song.

Britta's natural stage presence and sultry voice easily seduced her enthusiastic audience. The crowd was ecstatic. Doug helped Britta off the stage. Anna wiped away tears of happiness as she looked at Britta who was positively glowing. She was also impressed with Doug's piano playing. He was very good.

Britta and Lenny laughed together as the club owner sent over another bottle of champagne to their table. Doug asked Anna if she would like to find a quieter spot in the city. She wanted to go with him but was hesitant to leave Britta.

"Oh, let her stay. You can't mother her forever. After all, she is enjoying Lenny's company, and he will see that she gets home safely. She is twenty-one today," said Doug.

Anna checked with Britta to make sure it was all right for them to separate.

Lenny looked at Anna.

"She'll be fine. I will make sure she gets home safely."

She thanked Lenny who said he would be delighted to escort the birthday girl home. Britta kissed Anna goodbye on the cheek.

Doug patted Lenny on the shoulder, and Lenny mischievously gave Doug a knowing wink.

"It isn't like that this time," Doug insisted quietly, but Lenny just shook his head and laughed.

Together, they left the noisy club behind holding hands.

23

Late Night after the Jazz Club
April 7th

Knowing Britta would be dropped off safely at home, Doug and Anna could finally be alone—away from the noise of the club and the city. Still holding hands, they strolled slowly down a paved walkway that ran the length of the beach for as far as the eye could see. It was a starry night that seemed as if it might—thankfully—never end. The soft hiss of the surf made for a calming backdrop to their conversation.

Doug inquired about her gold ruble hanging from the gold chain around her neck.

"It is so beautiful and unusual, Anna. Why a Russian ruble?"

She told him,

"It was a present from my father on my fifteenth birthday. It's a flawed coin because of the askew bust of Czar Nicholas II," then said nothing else. She wanted to tell him more—but not quite yet.

Doug began to tell the story of why he was in Copenhagen—the real reason, though he did not reveal all the details.

"I am with the US Navy, and I'm in Europe to provide a plan for the safety and exit for Americans overseas in case this war escalates."

Anna's heart beat faster at his honesty. With each word she felt closer to him, not just because of how he looked, but because she recognized the essence of his character.

"I think you are an extraordinary man, Doug," Anna confided.

Suddenly, he turned to her.

"I never thought I would feel this way. I feel as if time has stopped. All that matters in this world is that we are together." He stopped speaking, having run out of words to express his profound, unexpected delight in meeting Anna.

Anna so wanted him to finish what he was saying. Instead, he softly caressed the side of her face. A deep blush bloomed on her cheek. He kissed her lightly on the lips. She seemed to float off the ground.

"I am sorry for being so forward," he said. She almost replied but instead kissed him back. She did not want this night to end.

It was a passionate poignant moment of hope for two searching souls.

24

Anna's Townhouse
April 7th

Anna invited Doug into her home when he dropped her off, but he resisted. He wanted to get back to the hotel to make sure his message had gotten through to Washington. The Danish had fewer than a hundred obsolete planes divided between the Navy and land forces of only eight hundred men. He knew from the information he had already gathered that an invasion was unavoidable at this point. The question was when?

He stood with Anna at her doorstep. They stared intensely into each other's eyes, two hearts that understood each other intuitively. They wanted to kiss again, but they resisted. It would heighten their excitement for tomorrow. Anna closed the door, and Doug walked down the walkway of her townhouse with a big smile on his face. He quickly turned around, ran back and knocked on her door again.

As soon as she opened the door, he gathered her in his arms and kissed her. His senses reeled as he felt her body melt into his. Consumed in flames, Doug felt completely connected to her. Anna and Doug backed urgently into her townhouse, then into her bedroom, as they passionately kissed one another.

Doug stopped and asked her,

"Are you sure?"

Anna gently pulled him toward the bed. She brought her face close to his. The passion in her eyes was all he saw.

"Don't I look sure?" Anna whispered, her lips just a breath away from his own.

He said, "I've fallen…" The rush was burning through his veins like a drug.

She smiled and, in a teasingly feminine gesture, slid her dress slowly off her shoulders onto the floor.

On Anna's bedroom wall, the light of the moon shone through the window, casting a silhouette on the bedroom wall.

25

April 8th, Early Morning

In bed, Doug and Anna lay next to one another and talked in a soft, soul-binding way about their different worlds.

Holding her in his arms, he brushed a wisp of hair from her forehead and softly said,

"I will be leaving Copenhagen to go to Paris this week, but I will return the first chance I get."

Anna, earnestly disappointed, responded,

"I understand this is important." Anna bit her lower lip. "Doug?" and hesitated for a moment.

"May I show you something concerning the formula I told you about before you leave? I don't normally share my research work, but for whatever reason, my instincts are telling me to share this with you, and I trust you to keep it secret."

Doug nodded and added,

"Anna, with my heart and soul, I will protect and guard your secret with my life. You have my promise." He was flattered that Anna confided in him.

Anna said,

"Please wait a moment." She reached under her bed for the shoebox hidden under the floorboard that contained the music box and the serum.

I need to share this with him, she thought. *I am not sure why I am doing this right now, but perhaps it's a matter of trusting in the laws of the universe. I believe with all my heart that I was not only meant to figure out this formula, but that I was also meant to share it with Doug. If something should happen to me...* She shrugged off the thought.

She confided in Doug.

"It took literally two years to unravel the molecular sequencing in order to be able to attempt to reproduce it. This is a complex series of mathematical sequencing. Without the final set of instructions," she said, "I would not know how to unravel it again, and as of yet, we still have not reproduced it."

She held back a bit, deciding not to tell Doug that those instructions were in the ruble she had made into a necklace that was hanging from the same chain that held her pentacle star. She opened the music box and showed him the tiny vial of liquid.

Doug held up the vial, looked at it and asked,

"Why is this serum hidden in a music box if it can save lives? Shouldn't this be locked up in the lab or somewhere safer than here?"

Anna explained,

"While much good can come from it, the serum is volatile in composition—the smallest mistake or an improper mixture could easily make it a deadly substance." She confessed, "Even when I took a big chance giving it to Britta, I feared it might not work, but I had nothing to lose either. In the wrong hands, it could be the deadliest chemical agent known to man. It is a water-based matrix. If chemically manipulated and put in the water supply, it could literally wipe out life on this planet. No one would think to look for it in the hidden compartment of a music box."

She explained further.

"The serum has the chemical composition to restore any damaged cell to its original healthy state, thereby curing many diseases. It basically neutralizes the effect of any toxins, but it could also be manipulated chemically to be a deadly agent. I am concerned that—in times such as these—the wrong person might get hold of it and use it to harm others." Anna did not add that she distrusted Dr. Spelman.

Doug remained silent, contemplating her words and the significance of what she had just shared with him. Though Doug did not admit it out loud, he understood what Anna meant. She had discovered the master switch that man had been searching for since the beginning of time, and many governments and organizations, including his own, would kill to acquire it, and possibly kill Anna in their quest to obtain it.

Anna looked into his eyes searchingly for his response as she returned the vial to the music box and its hiding place. Doug gently took Anna's hand and kissed it. Their mutual attraction grew stronger and stronger as they shared their deepest secrets and fears. Doug thanked his lucky stars that he had made the trip to Dr. Cunningham's home that morning. For the first time since learning of his father's identity, Doug was glad his father was alive.

She urged him to get up and get dressed. Anna put on her robe and, with a smile, took his hand and led him up the stairs to the roof of her townhouse. They sat watching the moon and stars in magical silence. Anna leaned against Doug, and he embraced her warm body, enjoying her softness in his arms. Anna shared with Doug the theory of how sitting under a full moon centers the liquids in a person's body just as the moon affects the gravitational tides, and how her mother used to make her and Britta sit under a full moon for twenty minutes every month.

Anna's head rested comfortably on Doug's shoulder. The twinkling stars as well as the glittering lights of Copenhagen and the ocean beyond were a breathtaking sight.

Anna seductively looked at Doug through smoky eyes, her voice huskier now, and whispered,

"Never for one minute for the rest of my life will I ever forget this moment in time with you. I know now that love can be created in a single instant."

Doug swallowed hard as he felt her words resonate down to the depths of his heart, knowing they would be permanently engraved in his memory. He looked at her. Forgetting everything but her, he said in a low, resonating voice,

"I am the luckiest man in the world to be here with you."

For the first time in his daredevil life, he worried about his own mortality. He also feared for Anna's. To lose her now would be worse than death. He never realized until this moment the intense bond that could unite two hearts. He had fallen in love.

◆　◆　◆　◆　◆　◆　◆　◆　◆　◆

They were both suddenly plunged from their dreams as they heard a loud crash of glass breaking the silence of the night, startling both of them. Anna heard Britta swear and groan. She realized that Britta had entered downstairs, attempting to tiptoe quietly so as not to disturb Anna. Britta did not realize Doug was there.

Anna ran downstairs. Britta had accidentally bumped into a glass vase in the hallway, which had shattered on the floor. She had cut her finger on a sharp edge of the glass as she tried to clean it up, but the blood had clotted immediately. Anna remembered a time when Britta's blood flow would barely slow for hours, and with each cut finger or knee, the possibility existed that Britta could bleed to death.

The serum had worked! The sisters shared a look of secret understanding between them.

Doug came running downstairs behind Anna from the rooftop and greeted Britta, who coldly dismissed him. Doug ignored her rudeness, attributing it to the champagne, and offered to help clean up the broken glass.

Anna scolded,

"Britta, please be careful not to cut yourself again. I'll get some bandages."

Britta responded rather flippantly,

"What's the difference? I'll be fine," as she flopped onto the sitting-room couch.

Anna started to bandage her hand and Britta dryly asked, "So how much do you think this formula is worth?"

"Shhh, it is not that easy, and you know it," Anna reminded her.

"The formula must stay a secret or dreadful things could happen. Britta, do you think that perhaps you had too much champagne? Where have you and Lenny been all night?"

As Britta went up the stairs, laughing she responded,

"We went to a strip club."

Anna laughed, and glanced at Doug somewhat embarrassed and said, "I think Britta has a good sense of humor."

Doug did not respond, thinking *What the hell was that buster thinking taking a twenty-one-year-old girl to a strip club?*

At the doorway to the townhouse now in the wee hours of the morning, Doug kissed Anna goodbye. He said,

"Lets meet for dinner later this evening. I have some business that I must attend to with Lenny in the afternoon, but I will meet you after that. Is seven o'clock all right?"

Anna smiled and nodded in agreement.

♦ ♦ ♦ ♦ ♦ ♦ ♦ ♦ ♦

As Doug's taxi pulled away, Lukas and Finn observed the exchange from their dark car across the street from Anna's townhouse. They had been sitting there watching for quite some time. Lukas was badly bruised, and Finn took a strong drag on a cigarette. Anna never noticed them as she waved goodbye to Doug. She closed the door and locked it, mindful of the serum hidden under the floorboard of the house.

◆ ◆ ◆ ◆ ◆ ◆ ◆ ◆ ◆ ◆

Before going to bed, Anna checked on Britta who was fast asleep. Anna sat on the edge of her sister's bed. *We are such stuff as dreams are made of, rounded with a little sleep,* she thought, remembering Shakespeare's famous line. Britta stirred and half opened her eyes.

Anna asked, "Did you have a nice birthday?"

Britta smiled very sleepily. "It was wonderful."

"Yes, it was. How is your finger?"

Britta held out her hand, the cut had healed.

As Britta turned over to go back to sleep, Anna sat watching for a moment, happy that Britta was doing so well. She thought about her magical evening with Doug. She had fallen in love with the most wonderful man.

As Anna went downstairs to turn the sitting room light off, she remembered the bit of torn paper from her research notebook that had slipped into the side of the couch cushions. She pulled up the cushion. It was no longer there. *It must be here somewhere. I'll look later when it's light out,* she thought, exhausted.

◆ ◆ ◆ ◆ ◆ ◆ ◆ ◆ ◆ ◆

26

Copenhagen Café
April 8th

Early the next morning, Doug and Lenny had ordered a hearty breakfast in a busy Copenhagen café with Alistair Gordon who was dressed in a business suit and looking very much like a banker.

"I almost did not recognize you," Lenny joked as he shoved a piece of sausage in his mouth.

"I was looking for a stewardess, a German officer or a bum."

Doug looked at Alistair and said,

"Hey, thanks for saving our asses last night."

Alistair picked up his coffee cup and said,

"I leave you alone for one night and you pick a fight with the Nazis?" Both Doug and Lenny grinned sheepishly.

They discussed the specifics of the deal they had made with Dumas to allow safe housing for Americans and their allies abroad during the impending wartime. Doug revealed to Alistair a list of other safe houses with passwords and locations attached. They also discussed the communications system that Dumas had set up in Paris. Alistair was already aware of this.

Alistair began,

"We have some very serious problems going on here—there are seven code-breaking organizations in Hitler's Reich, including The Foreign Office, The Navy, The Army, The Luftwaffe and various others." Inhaling on his cigarette again, he paused, blowing the smoke out in tiny rings again.

"The most efficient is the B-Dienst—they have already cracked the Royal Navy Administrative Code used by our enlisted sailors—but now the B-Dienst (Beobachtungsdienst) has also cracked the Naval Cipher which is used only by British Officers for top-secret communications. Given rumors of a German invasion here, this is compromising communications with our naval fleet in these waters."

Doug nodded, remembering his training a few years ago in code operations at Bletchley Park in England. He knew the Americans had been using a device called the SIGABA, and the British were using Type–X. Both encryption systems were based on the enigma model which used a five-rotor system.

Alistair continued,

"We already have a good relationship with Dumas and his lads, which is very valuable. However, our immediate priority is the increased radio chatter that is emanating from the German frontier. An invasion is imminent. The Danes have only two coastal vessels dating to 1906 and 1918, seventeen torpedo boats, twelve submarines, no tanks and less than one hundred obsolete aircraft. The Germans won't stand a chance if we are here, but we have to be able to communicate with our naval fleet.

"Doug, can you get a message to Washington and have them relay this information to London? If we go through your channels, it should be secure. Everything here is compromised," said Alistair. As he leaned forward, he whispered in a low voice, "Hitler knows that there is a vast amount of gold bullion and coins in these bank vaults. The most immediate need is to get these assets out of Norway and Denmark as soon as possible."

Lenny, who had been busy consuming his eggs and sausage, now interjected.

"It would behoove Hitler to get his hands on this gold since he needs the capital to fuel his war machine." Doug nodded in agreement.

Then Lenny asked Doug about his meeting with his friend.

Doug hesitated before replying.

"Oh, right. A Dr. Cunningham, a family friend who knew my mother years ago." After a short pause he added, "Before I was born."

Alistair, whose ears were quick to pick up Doug's ambivalence about the man, interjected.

"Hello there, boys. The good doctor, Johann Cunningham, is one of us. He helps us run communications and provides great cover. He is well known and respected by all. The Germans like him as well since he worked over there. How is it you know him?"

Doug answered evasively,

"He was a friend of my mother's, some sort of distant relative."

"Did he mention his involvement in any of this?" asked Alistair.

"I don't suppose I gave him a chance," replied Doug ruefully, not wanting to go into any further detail.

"Well, keep him in mind if you run into any trouble. We've had a jolly good time sending the wrong data to the Germans through him, although there is some question about his involvement with this new drug, penicillin. Do you know anything about it?"

Doug and Lenny responded that as far as they knew, only the UK and the US scientists had been able to make high-grade penicillin and only in very small quantities.

Alistair leaned forward again and whispered,

"Apparently, yesterday we found out that Hitler's doctor is trying to obtain some of this drug. Penicillin is meant to be an extremely restricted substance. Hitler's interest in obtaining this makes us suspect that he might be sick."

Doug's brain instantly processed the news, and both he and Lenny became uneasy as they remembered giving a small, good faith sample of penicillin to Dumas at the chateau.

The men talked a little more about the jazz club and the fight with the Gestapo thugs.

Alistair looked at them very seriously and, in a low voice, cautioned Doug and Lenny.

"Those boys are part of the Sicherheitsdienst, the sister arm of the Gestapo, and are deadly assassins. We have been keeping a close eye on them. We suspect they are interested in the research scientists at the Institute. Do not think for one minute that your encounter was accidental, and now you had better believe you are on their 'To Do' hit list."

Doug did not mention Anna. They talked for just a few minutes more as Alistair was in a hurry to get to another appointment. He would talk to Lenny about taking Britta to a strip club at a more appropriate time.

"Ta, we'll be in touch, gents. Meanwhile, I would strongly suggest you leave Copenhagen while you still can."

The three men shook hands and went their separate ways.

27

Late Morning, Anna's Townhouse, Copenhagen
April 8th

Anna awoke suddenly. It was late morning, and she had overslept. She heard women's voices from downstairs. Rubbing her sleepy eyes and yawning, she descended the stairs. Turning the corner, she found Britta having coffee in the sitting room with their mutual friend, Margo.

" Good morning, Margo. How nice of you to visit. I'm sorry, I'm afraid I overslept." Anna said with a faint grin.

Britta was quick to reply,

"Anna, Margo brought me a birthday bouquet and has come to say goodbye. She doesn't feel safe in Copenhagen anymore."

Margo, a longtime neighbor, was considerably chic, willowy rather than gaunt. Her auburn hair neatly pinned and coiffed and her thin lips stained with bright red lipstick, she rose to her feet to kiss Anna on the cheek.

"Yes, Anna, it's true. I am leaving today for Paris to stay with family who are living near the Champs-Élysées. I urge you and Britta to come with me because I believe we are all in danger." With worry clouding her hazel eyes, she inquired of Anna, "What are they saying at the Institute?"

With a chill of foreboding and goose bumps on her arms, Anna calmly responded,

"Margo, we are all being careful with our research, but no one seems overly concerned that Denmark could be in trouble," as she walked to the kitchen to get a cup of coffee.

Britta teasingly added,

"Based on last night and the promise of new love, Anna is too hopeful about her future to want to leave Copenhagen at this time, Margo. We met two dashing American men last night," Britta said as she winked at Margo.

Margo, rolling her eyes, glimpsed a scrap of paper on the floor by the side of the couch. She picked it up and turned it over, and seeing nothing but a scribbled picture of a triangle, she decided it was nothing important but a piece of torn paper. She turned it back over and wrote out her contact information in Paris. Since Anna was in the kitchen, she handed it to Britta.

"Here is my phone number in Paris in case either of you ever want to visit or are forced to leave."

Britta smugly replied,

"Oh, Margo, you are a reactionist," as she shoved the piece of paper in her pocket.

Anna returned to the sitting room with a cup of coffee and set it down on the table, remaining quiet. The information she had learned during her conversation with Doug led her to believe Margo might be right.

Margo glanced at her watch anxiously.

"Oh, I must be going or I'm going to miss my train." She stood up, buttoned her canary yellow coat and hugged both women goodbye.

Once Margo left, Anna went to clean up the coffee cups and straighten the cushions on the couch. Anna felt uneasy but Britta seemed unaffected by Margo's speculations and sudden departure. Glancing at the ashes in the fireplace, Anna suddenly remembered the missing scrap of paper. She asked Britta,

"By the way, did you see a torn bit of paper on the couch yesterday?"

Britta shrugged on her way up the stairs.

"I have no idea what you are talking about," and closed her bedroom door.

♦ ♦ ♦ ♦ ♦ ♦ ♦ ♦ ♦ ♦

28

Morning in Another Part of Copenhagen
April 8th

Dr. Spelman sat in front of a mahogany desk at The Bank of Denmark.

The banker, a stern bearded man, walked in and shook Dr. Spelman's hand. "Good morning. How can I be of assistance to you today, Dr. Spelman?"

Dr. Spelman looked across directly at the banker now seated behind his desk and said, "I want to transfer the funds from one of my personal accounts into a new account. I am concerned my account number and personal information may have been breached."

The banker looked at him. "Breached? Not at this bank, I assure you."

Dr. Spelman said, "These are dangerous times. One can never be too sure."

The banker nodded seriously and pulled out his fountain pen as he inquired, "How much are you looking to transfer?"

Dr. Spelman replied, "One million Reichsmarks into Swiss currency to be forwarded to a Swiss account."

The banker paused in his writing, hiding his surprise, and looked up suspiciously at Dr. Spelman. "I assume you have proper identification?"

Dr. Spelman pulled out a folder with cards and papers and handed them to the banker.

The banker looked over the papers for what seemed longer than necessary, then finally granted Dr. Spelman his request. "Well, everything seems to be in order. Sign here and here."

The banker took back the signed papers and began to fill them out.

Dr. Spelman, organized his papers, and placed them back in his folder, when a train ticket fell onto the desk. The banker glanced at the ticket before Dr. Spelman could snatch it up.

It read 'Le Gard Du Nord, Paris'.

"Is there anything else I can do for you today, Dr. Spelman?" he asked, deciding not to mention the ticket.

"No, thank you. I'm leaving today on holiday. Good day." With his hat still on to cover the bandage on his head, Dr. Spelman stood up, nodded and quickly left the bank.

As the banker watched Dr. Spelman leave, he picked up the phone and started dialing.

29

Early Afternoon in Copenhagen
April 8th

Anna and Britta were in the tiny courtyard out in the back of their townhouse. Linens hung on a clothesline, drying in the late morning sun. Anna confessed to Britta her growing attachment to Doug.

"We are having dinner tonight, Britta. Will you be all right?"

Britta laughed.

"Of course, I will be. But what about you? No hanky-panky."

Anna blushed. Anna was unable to properly describe or even understand what was going on between her and Doug. It was unlike anything she had ever experienced. Britta began dancing and dragged Anna into her swirling movement as both girls laughed.

As Anna prepared to leave for her dinner date with Doug, she walked over to Britta and, with a warm hug, said,

"I don't know what I would have done if anything ever happened to you."

"But I'm fine now. Where is the rest of it in case we need more?" Britta asked while she sipped her coffee.

"I have hidden the formula in the ruble—but never tell anyone I'll tell you more when I get home later.!" confided Anna as she wrapped a shawl around her pink cocktail dress.

Their sisterly bond was unbreakable.

Or so Anna thought.

♦ ♦ ♦ ♦ ♦ ♦ ♦ ♦ ♦ ♦

Across the street that evening, Lukas and Finn were once again on stakeout outside the townhouse, unnoticeable. They walked toward the building. Britta was inside, alone and unsuspecting.

They had watched as Anna left with Doug for their dinner date. Lukas and Finn were about to enter the townhouse when suddenly a car pulled up outside. Quickly hiding behind the bushes, they recognized the Russian club owner and were puzzled by his presence. He knocked on the door and was quickly welcomed inside by Britta. After a short while, he left.

It was now getting late, and they still had to get inside the townhouse to find the missing part of the formula Dr. Spelman was so certain Anna had discovered. Just then another man walked up, the other American.

"I want to kill him just as we should have at the club," growled Finn.

Lukas held his finger to his lips and whispered,

"Not now. Later."

Lukas and Finn watched as Britta and Lenny left. Now was the time for them to go in.

♦ ♦ ♦ ♦ ♦ ♦ ♦ ♦ ♦ ♦

30

Later that Evening
April 8th

"This night would set the stage for life and death to play out their respective parts, in a world where devastating wars that can destroy nations were a thought that existed in the mind of one single man."

Later, as the stars began to shimmer in the evening sky, Anna and Doug dined at a popular restaurant in downtown Copenhagen. Anna, elegantly dressed in a pink silk cocktail dress, with her hair up, sat across from Doug at a small table with a white linen tablecloth and two candles. She looked into Doug's green eyes as he raked his hand through his thick dark hair. His stitches from the accident with the horse's hooves were healing well, and the scar was barely noticeable.

The specks of gold from his green eyes glinted in the candlelight. His jaw line was strong. The small scar on his left temple only added to his masculinity.

As Doug wondered how Sean was doing, he leaned forward and, holding Anna's hand, told her the story of rescuing the boy from the mare's temper. Anna was drawn in even more by his compassion. Anna wanted to know what Paris was like, and Doug painted a very romantic portrait of the city while they ate a savory meal of pan-seared Baltic Sea flounder with remoulade, ice shrimp and white asparagus.

Anna said, "I'd like to visit someday. As a girl I used to pretend I was an artist in Montmartre, a place I only knew about from the stories my mother used to read to me as a child and from books I have read."

Doug asked her to share more stories about her mother with him and commented on her pentacle necklace. Being well read, he pointed out to Anna that her necklace had only five points, unlike the Star of David which has six. He told her it was designated the Pentateuch, the five books of Moses, and had had various names, including "The Druid's Root" and "The Witches' Star."

Anna listened intently, amazed at Doug's knowledge. He went on to say that to the followers of Pythagoras it was called the "Pentalpha," being composed of five interlaced A's, or Alphas.

"Of course, you know alpha is the first letter of the alphabet and the Pythagorean Theorem—the sum of the areas of the two squares on the legs equals the area of the square on the hypotenuse." He laughed easily, realizing Anna's knowledge in this probably exceeded his. "I studied a lot of geometry at MIT."

Anna was startled and shifted uncomfortably in her chair, avoiding Doug's eyes for a moment. *Surely he couldn't know that the protein structure of her molecular formula on the hidden microfilm started with Alpha.*

"Anna, if your mother gave you this, it was because she was passing on its universal wisdom and protection to you. In geometry, the pentacle is an elegant expression of the ratio phi which was considered by the Pythagoreans to express the truth about the hidden nature of existence. She must have been an amazing woman. I would have liked to have met her," continued Doug, smiling compassionately.

"My mother used to take me to a sulphur spring when I was a little girl. She knew so much about the herbs in the forest. That is how I was introduced to healing medicine. She believed there was, on this planet, a natural cure in the water or forests for anything that ails you. She strived to gain knowledge of and use the natural remedies placed on this earth by the Divine for our benefit.

"I remember falling as a little girl and she put this mudpack on my cut and bruised leg. Within a day, the cut was all better and had healed without a scar. She kept her notes all in one book with this pentacle star at the top of each page. It contained recipes for headache remedies, cold tonics and herbal baths. Ironically, the book is at Dr. Cunningham's house."

Doug looked at her curiously.

"Anna, I think I saw that notebook open on his desk that first day when I went to visit him. I didn't think that much about it because I was so surprised at his revelation. He also had a handmade pentacle that was framed."

"Oh, that was probably from my mother—she loved to crochet. They had corresponded for years and traded medicinal recipes back and forth, although they never met. My mother thought a cure could come from harvesting the mold on bread, and I believe that started Dr. Cunningham's interest in penicillin. At any rate he was partly responsible for helping me get into Oxford at a young age. They wouldn't let me live at the school, so I stayed with his Aunt Mary at his cottage. She was like a surrogate mother to me."

Anna added somberly "My mother died of pneumonia on a very cold winter's day in Russia. The town was snowed in for days with no medical assistance. Britta was only two years old."

"Doug, I tried to remember all the herbs and mixtures she used. I gave her one after the other, but I couldn't save her. I was only twelve years old, but I felt partly responsible for her death. Perhaps if I had paid more attention to her remedies, I could have saved her. That's why I went into medical research." Anna's eyes started to water, so she quickly changed the subject and asked Doug to tell her about America.

Having sensed her discomfort, Doug obliged her by telling funny stories of his escapades at his Massachusetts
boarding school. He told her about a game of truth-and-dare
his first week in school. He had opted for the dare to prove his
bravery, so his friends blindfolded him and led him into a
room he thought was the bathroom.

"Anna, you have to imagine this: they have me put my
hand in lukewarm water and they told me to squeeze
something. Well, it turned out it was a peeled banana in two
halves, but that's not what I thought it was, being blindfolded
and being taken to what I thought was the bathroom."

Doug laughed so easily it was contagious, and soon Anna
found herself laughing uncontrollably with him.

Anna and Doug were comfortable getting to know one
another. Anna's honesty and laughter continued to appeal to
him, so much so that he thought he might like to make love to
her right there in the restaurant. The magnetism between them
was almost visible to the naked eye. He laughed to himself at
the thought as Anna continued to tell her own story. But then
Anna's leg touched Doug's under the table.

31

The Eve of the Invasion of Denmark and Norway
Doug's Hotel, Copenhagen
April 8th

Doug and Anna, after having enjoyed a lovely candlelit dinner, returned to Doug's hotel for a nightcap. The French doors on Doug's suite were open and looked out on the lights of Copenhagen. Anna thought she saw fireworks, but before she could get the words out, Doug noticed in the distance pinpricks of light in the air. They appeared to be getting closer and closer as the seconds rolled by. Concern began to grow in Doug's eyes. He knew what he was looking at: fighter planes approaching at an inordinate speed with malice on their agenda.

Anna sensed his mood shift and asked,

"What's wrong, Doug?"

Suddenly, from the opposite direction, a fighter plane zoomed overhead seeming eerily close to the ground. Doug looked up—surveillance no doubt. Doug again looked at the approaching pinpricks of light, realizing they were bombs exploding in the distance. *The Luftwaffe has started the invasion.*

Suddenly, there was an urgent knock on the door. Doug took out his gun cautiously. As Doug opened the door, Lenny rushed in, quickly nodding to Anna.

"Doug, the Germans are invading and the British warships have mined the fjords of Norway to prevent the Swedish iron ore from getting to Germany. The Germans are retaliating. They are invading Norway and Denmark; all communications have been taken over, including the newspapers." Lenny showed Doug a message issued by the Germans.

"(Special Information) In order to counter British preparations to take away the neutrality of Denmark and Norway, German Wehrmacht has taken over armed defense of both nations."

Doug excused himself from Anna for a few minutes to meet with Lenny in his room across the hall. They needed to discuss their operation and communications setup.

As Anna continued to watch from the French doors of the hotel room, a sudden sense of panic spread through her. Tonight she had just worn the necklace, but now she took out the ruble and proceeded to put the pentacle inside, then slipped it on the fine gold chain around her neck. She reached for the phone to call Britta but put the receiver down as she remembered Lenny saying that all communications had been taken over.

"Doug, you must take Anna back to her home immediately," urged Lenny, "before we proceed to the airport."

"We are still neutral but we need to get out of here, and Anna is in danger here too. Also, the first thing they will do is bomb the airstrips," Doug reminded him.

Lenny nodded in agreement.

"You are right! It's probably too late to get to the airport. It'll be the first thing the Germans go after. I'll go with you and Anna to the townhouse to make sure Britta is all right."

"All right, Lenny, given that British Intelligence is compromised with that Venlo incident, I think we should split up. I will try to get the girls across to Paris or London. They will be safer there for now. After that, I will try to secure the immigration papers for the girls to come to the US with us, since I am certain Anna will not leave her sister behind."

Both men ran across the hall to get Anna from Doug's room and head to her townhouse.

♦ ♦ ♦ ♦ ♦ ♦ ♦ ♦ ♦ ♦

They had no idea that Lukas and Finn had entered Anna's townhouse in search of the formula. Frustrated at not finding anything, Lukas and Finn had ransacked the entire place.

The microfilm was not in the townhouse. It was in the ruble which Anna had with her. Racing with him back to the townhouse, Anna said to Doug, "See this ruble…" she held it in her hand for him to see. Anna never finished her sentence as running robbed her of the breath to speak.

Doug, not wanting to waste any time, said,

"Anna, later. We have to hurry." He grabbed her hand and rushed her down the street.

Anna, Doug and Lenny shouted for Britta in every nook and cranny of the townhouse, but she did not answer. The townhouse had been turned upside down. Someone had clearly been looking for something, and Anna suspected she knew what it was. She looked in Britta's room, but Britta was not there. Anna called fervently, "Britta, where are you?" She ran to her room, everything was overturned, but she quickly noticed the floorplank by her bed had not been disturbed.

Lenny called out from upstairs. "Check the courtyard. She might be out back."

As Anna stumbled into the courtyard calling Britta's name, she noticed a red splash of blood on one of the linens hanging from the clothesline that was blocking her view of the tiny courtyard. With mounting fear, Anna pushed the linens aside and fell to her knees screaming. A puddle of blood soaked the ground floor of the courtyard. Britta's arm was flung out in an unnatural position over her head, which was face down in blood.

Doug and Lenny rushed in right behind Anna. The white linens hanging on the clothesline brought a quick flashback to Doug, another moment from his childhood. He quickly picked Anna up and held her in his arms, shielding her from the gruesome sight. Lenny leaned over Britta and checked her pulse, shaking his head in dismay at Doug. He wiped the blood from her neck on one of the sheets.

"She's dead," Lenny said. Seeing Anna's panic and distress, he said, "I will take care of Britta. You two must make your escape now. Go on ahead to Paris or London and contact Dumas. I will try to get a message ahead to Dumas and Alistair and reconnect with you later. Go now—and hurry!"

Explosions could be heard in the distance. Doug knew the Germans would bomb the airports, bridges and major roads first. He also knew they must leave immediately. He hugged Anna and covered her eyes from the sight of Britta lying dead in the courtyard. He made her focus on him instead.

"Anna, look at me. In twenty minutes, this entire city will be swarming with men who will kill you without a second thought. We need to leave immediately."

Anna refused, her eyes filled with fear, as the tears rolled down her cheeks.

He refocused her eyes on his once again.

"Anna, please…"

She looked back toward the courtyard as Doug led her out. Lenny had covered Britta with a sheet. The blood was everywhere. Anna ran up the brick courtyard stairs but slipped; her hands broke her fall. Her hands were covered with blood. As she screamed, the sound stuck in her throat. Doug caught her and put his hand over her eyes.

He lifted her by the arms to her feet, but Anna could barely stand. She was in a haze of shock and sorrow. He took her into her bedroom where she removed the shoebox from under the floorboard beneath her bed. She took out the small music box which contained the vial of serum and ruble in the secret compartment. She grabbed the glass vial from the music box and threw it to the floor, feeling nothing but anger and despair. Doug, in one swift catlike move, caught the vial before it hit the floor and put it in his pocket.

"Anna, what are you doing? This is your legacy, your discovery. You can't just throw it away."

Anna, completely devastated by the sudden loss of her sister, felt as if her own child had just died. "Doug, they were looking for me, whoever they are, not Britta. She is innocent. Britta's murder is my fault."

Doug lifted Anna to her feet once again. His calm exterior and training went into autopilot as he reached into her closet for some boots, warm slacks and a thick, wool sweater. "Here," he instructed Anna as he handed her the clothes, "change into them immediately." She changed out of her pink cocktail dress and was coherent enough to remember her music box. Doug put the vial back in it and put in a leather pouch. As she put on a large overcoat, he quickly tied the strings of the pouch to the inside pocket of her overcoat.

Doug understood what Britta's murder meant; the Germans, or someone, considered Anna and her formula worth killing for. They would stop at nothing to get their hands on her. He could not do anything more for Britta, but he could save Anna if they hurried. They needed to flee Copenhagen.

"Anna, let's go, we need to get out of Denmark immediately." Doug grabbed her hand and rushed her out of the townhouse.

32

Together, they ran swiftly onto the dark, empty street and zigzagged through back alleyways until they got close to Doug's hotel. Doug practically dragged Anna as she stumbled along blindly, tears spilling down her face. He suddenly slowed down when he noticed a flurry of activity a few yards in front of him. He quickly pulled Anna into the shadows. There was much unexpected activity going on at the bank across the street. Doug stopped in the shadows to assess the situation.

The men were not in German uniforms, but plain workers' clothes. In the complete darkness of the alley behind the bank, trucks were being loaded with large oak barrels, the kind of barrels that were used to store fine wine. By the grunts of the dozen darkly clad men lifting them, the barrels seemed to be quite heavy. Several casks were stacked in a neat row.

Have the Germans caught on to the gold reserves already and are raiding the bank? The thought raced through Doug's mind.

Out of nowhere, a man with a knit mask roughly grabbed Doug and covered his mouth with a hard-gloved hand, pulling him further into the shadows of the poorly lit alleyway. As the mysterious man was ready to fire a bullet into Doug's skull, Doug felt the cold steel on his temple.

Shit, he thought. He would ordinarily knock this man on the ground in a swift martial arts move, but he was concerned about Anna. In a surprise move, the man took a quick glance at Anna who was still in shock, and then took a second look at Doug. He removed his weapon from Doug's head and put it away in the holster strapped behind his back.

"Doug, bloody hell, you jackass! You gave me a real fright coming up on us that way. I almost put a bullet through your skull. Give us a hand, will you? We are moving the bullion reserves out of the city before the Germans get their hands on them. These are the last few barrels to load on the trucks before we have it all."

"Alistair, I need help to get Anna out of Copenhagen immediately. Someone broke into Anna's place and killed Britta. Whoever it was tore the place apart looking for something."

Alistair looked at Anna and then back at Doug, noticing Anna's ashen face for the first time.

"You can both ride in the truck with me. You had best get her out of here while you can. We'll talk on the way. Obviously, her research is valuable to them, so she is at risk. Cunningham is here. He will help her as well."

The men were working with great speed in an assembly line. Some were inside the open bank vault. They formed a line that stretched out in three-foot intervals, passing the gold in buckets, packing it into the barrels, and then passing those into the trucks, all without making a sound. The complete silence was eerie against the backdrop of the still-roaring bombers. At the far end of the line, Doug saw Dr. Cunningham issuing orders quietly and in complete control of the dangerous situation.

The men finished loading the trucks and drove away from the bank as discreetly as possible without conversation, not even a whisper. They left their truck headlights off as an extra precaution to avoid alerting any surveillance aircraft. An ambush on the road would be disastrous. Anna, still in shock, was adrift in her own world, staring out the window. She seemed unaware of the chaos swirling around her. All she could think of was Britta's body lying in a pool of blood.

Doug and Alistair discussed their escape options with Cunningham.

"Which way would be the best route out of the country? Do we try to navigate the Oresund Straits to Sweden?" There were two issues to be decided as the Germans could be expected to aggressively pursue both the gold, once they discovered it was gone, and Anna, once they discovered she was missing.

Cunningham replied, "The German warships supporting the ground troops will make passage through there impossible. We will have to find another way. Doug, I'm glad you and Anna are all right. I am sorry about Britta. I promise you we will get to the bottom of this." His gaze softened as he glanced over at Anna.

Anna looked at him with sorrowful eyes. They were not yet safe at all.

As Doug listened to Dr. Cunningham intelligently referring to information that was highly classified, he suddenly realized that Cunningham must be one of the primary leaders of the British Special Operations Executive. He further supported Doug's assumption by commenting on special classified information being transmitted to him from London.

"I have received coded instructions from London to meet a Royal Navy ship bound for Scotland. This indicates that Operation Weserübung has begun. Denmark and Norway are being invaded and communication to these countries have been taken over completely by the Germans, including all radio. The Luftwaffe has taken control of the air. We need to get the gold out now before any troops land!"

Alistair suggested to Cunningham, "Maybe we should try for Helsingør, since it is only about forty kilometers north of Copenhagen, and cross the narrow straits to Helsingborg into Sweden."

Cunningham shook his head.

"Nazi warships would make that crossing equally impossible."

It seemed the Germans had locked down the possibility of traveling directly by sea with their blockades.

Finally, the small convoy decided to try to escape from Copenhagen's island by heading west, hoping to make the Danish mainland. They would travel southwest, first to Roskilde, and then Ringsted before heading west to Slagelse of the Store Bælt—the straits that separate their island from the island of Fry to the west. It promised to be a journey of about one hundred miles.

Cunningham looked at Alistair and Doug.

"I am sure the Nazis now want to capture Anna and acquire her research. No doubt, Dr. Spelman has told them she has discovered something. They will be adamant in continuing their search for her."

Anna in her despair looked at Dr. Cunningham.

"But I told Dr. Spelman I couldn't make any progress with our research."

Dr. Cunningham replied,

"Obviously, Anna, he didn't believe you. Or he wanted to target you to take the pressure off of himself. Never liked that man."

Alistair added, "They will also be interested in discovering Doug's movements since his confrontation with the Gestapo's secret assassins believing that he may have access to Anna's research."

Both Anna and Doug were now in danger, and Dr. Cunningham felt they would be safer making their escape separately from the gold, which would be a prime target. He knew it wouldn't be long before the Germans realized the gold was gone.

Dr. Cunningham commented to Alistair and Doug,

"The American Embassy in Copenhagen is compromised; it won't be safe to go there, and it's too dangerous to return to the capital. The Germans will be landing at Gedser and moving north and they will probably take the two airfields at Aalborg."

Alistair agreed, adding,

"We must make it to the west end of the island before dawn. It would be best to cross the straits while it is still dark. We will need to stay on interior roads to avoid the German army as it moves inland from their landing beaches." Alistair and Cunningham knew they could not risk making any contact with the Royal Navy at this point. There were too many German warships to contend with. All communications were compromised.

Alistair and Cunningham were intent on delivering their cargo of gold bullion and coins to England. If they moved quickly enough, they might be able to stay one step ahead of the invading army. They reasoned that the Germans could not yet have had enough time to set up roadblocks and circulate descriptions of those they wanted to apprehend. They would travel in disguise and quickly, before daylight; the foggy night would work in their favor.

◆ ◆ ◆ ◆ ◆ ◆ ◆ ◆ ◆ ◆

33

Night Escape on Swedish Freighter
April 9th

The convoys of trucks arrived safely at the docks. Doug, Dr. Cunningham and Alistair negotiated with the captains of various fishing boats to take them and their cargo across the strait to the island of Fry.

The gold was loaded into several boats, and Dr. Cunningham and Alistair split up. Even if one was taken, with luck and strategy most of the gold would make it to England. In the best-case scenario, both Cunningham and Alistair would arrive safely with their cargo intact to the Royal Navy ship bound for Scotland.

Anna and Doug negotiated for one of the smaller boats. Dr. Cunningham walked over, gave Anna a big hug and shook Doug's hand as they were about to board the vessel.

"Doug, Godspeed, son, and take good care of her. We'll meet up in London. Try to make it to Southampton, and I'll get an escort vehicle for you. Send a message as soon as you can. Meanwhile, I will contact Washington the first chance I get. Take this map with you and if you get to Rotterdam or Southampton, make contact and we will arrange to get you to London."

Cunningham handed Doug a small fly and said,

"This is a tracking device that works on a radio frequency. Should something happen, London Headquarters will be able to find you. Attach it to the underside of your shirt, but be aware it does not work in water."

Doug took it and immediately recognized it from his visit to Cunningham's house. "Thank you," replied Doug as he attached it to his shirt.

Doug navigated the boat out of the murky dock while Anna huddled down in the hull. The boat smelled pungent, like bait and wet rope. Doug saw a man's cap and handed it to Anna along with a life vest.

Several miles out to sea, a dark mass loomed in the foggy night on a direct collision course with their small vessel. Doug fired off three flares to alert the freighter, but the freighter continued towards them. There was nothing that could be done. The freighter passed, narrowly missing them, but the wake overturned the small boat and catapulted Anna and Doug into the icy water.

They clung to the one part of their fishing vessel that remained afloat. The deep fog made for poor visibility; Doug could barely make out the markings of the freighter.

"I can't make out the markings, but it's clearly the freighter that capsized us. Obviously, they didn't see the flares. You're not hurt, are you?" Anna shook her head, her teeth chattering from the cold water.

The night-duty guard aboard the freighter saw the flares and raised the alarm. Chaos ensued on the freighter as the crew rushed around. The ship came to a stop several miles beyond their location. A lifeboat was dropped into the water to rescue any survivors.

Doug shouted,

"Here! Anna, they're coming."

Shivering from the icy water, Anna and Doug were helped on board the freighter from the lifeboat. Anna's clothes were so heavy with water she was dragged to the deck when they boarded. The night watchman approached with blankets and hot coffee. Doug helped Anna remove her outer clothing and wrapped a blanket around her, careful to keep an eye on her overcoat.

The ship was a Swedish-registered vessel, *The Wesser*, bound for the port of Rostock in Germany. They gratefully wrapped their fingers around the warm cups in the captain's office and snuggled inside the warm wool blankets. The captain walked to a small bar in the corner of his quarters and took out a bottle of whiskey.

"What nationality are you? Do you speak Swedish?" asked the captain in Swedish as he offered Doug a glass filled with whiskey adding, "My name is Captain Hans."

Doug replied,

"We are American. Do you speak French or English? Thank you for rescuing us," Doug said as he took a big gulp of the warm liquid before offering the glass to Anna.

She took a small sip and shuddered as the liquid burned her throat.

Speaking broken English, the captain continued.

"Our ship is named *The Wesser*. We just picked up cargo in Norway and then stopped at Göteborg, Sweden, to take on some high-grade iron ore for German manufacturing plants."

Doug's mind raced ahead. He pulled Anna aside and whispered as the captain walked back to replace the bottle in his bar.

"This change of plans could be even better. Going to Germany will throw everyone off track. No one looking for you will think to look for you there. Rostock is probably the best port of call for us. From there, we can find our way over land to Holland. My trainer, O'Grady, can meet up with us in Belgium, and then we can make our way to Paris."

Anna nodded sadly, not caring. She was still grieving over Britta. In addition, she was wet, cold and tired from their boating escapade.

Captain Hans began to question Doug and Anna. He was suspicious of what circumstances might have placed them in the middle of the straits. "What were you doing directly in the shipping lanes of the straits at this time of night?"

Doug answered,

"We are visiting from America and were going to spend a week visiting some cousins at a nearby island. My wife Anna and I were offered a boat at a reasonable price. We had no idea we were in any danger. We thought it would be a reasonably safe and short journey. Somehow in all of the fog, we got off course."

Captain Hans looked suspiciously at their left hands and noticed that neither of them had a wedding band on. He also noticed an expensive Swiss watch on Doug's wrist. *Surely they could have afforded a more luxurious way to travel other than on a fishing boat. And where is the boat captain?* He wondered.

Captain Hans was clearly not convinced of their story. *Yes*, he thought wryly, *something stinks in the state of Denmark*, and surreptitiously, on his return to the wheelhouse, he radioed ahead to Rostock to alert the German authorities. Captain Hans ordered a crewman to keep watch on Doug and Anna in the cabin below where they would rest.

They were escorted below to the first-mate's cabin. He was evicted and gathered his belongings to go share a cabin with the second mate. Before he left, he located some dry clothes for Anna and Doug to change into which were more dry than they were clean. Once alone, Anna removed the pouch from her drenched outer coat and tied it securely to the inside of her clothing.

Doug and Anna looked at each other, reading each other's minds, as they questioned whether to trust Captain

Hans. They both had a bad feeling about him. The addition of the armed watchman outside their cabin door did nothing to dispel their doubt. Doug paced the cabin, concerned.

"Doug," began Anna slowly still shivering,

"As I was leaning over the stern of the boat, I wanted to take all my grief over Britta and the responsibility of this formula and just throw it overboard…like watching a big heavy weight sink slowly to the bottom, out of sight, out of mind, out of heart, forever. No more pain."

Doug's arms closed protectively around her.

♦ ♦ ♦ ♦ ♦ ♦ ♦ ♦ ♦ ♦

34

April 10th, 2:00 AM

After some time had passed, Anna knocked on the cabin door. The crewman guarding the door outside opened it.

Anna asked politely,

"Excuse me. I need to use the bathroom. I am feeling a bit ill." She was allowed to go to the restroom without the guard.

She worked her way up to the main deck. The actions of the captain had puzzled her greatly. *Why has Captain Hans posted a guard when he was told that we are American and neutral?* She decided to use the opportunity to look around the ship while nobody was paying much attention to her. The crewman assigned to watch Doug and Anna had remained below to keep an eye on Doug who was considered more of a threat by Captain Hans.

Anna wandered around the deck, struggling for her sea legs, breathing in deeply the fresh sea air. It was refreshing to leave the stale air of the cabin. The night fog had cleared up, and the stars were on full display. She walked near the bridge where she overheard a conversation between the captain and one of his officers. Staying hidden, she listened to him talking to one of his men.

"I have been informed by the authorities in Rostock that the woman onboard matches the description of the scientist the Gestapo have been seeking. They may also be working with

163

British Intelligence. I am concerned about our cargo being discovered by her and her husband. If they see what we are carrying and report us to the Brits, we will be considerably less able to maneuver across the lines and trade so actively with all parties. This conflict between countries can make us rich. It is imperative we keep them closely guarded. I don't trust them. Radio Rostock authorities and see what they say."

Upon hearing this, Anna's anger was now fully inflamed. She quietly took a stairwell below deck. She believed it was the Nazis who had ransacked her townhouse and killed Britta in their search for her formula. Determined to avenge Britta's death, Anna made a silent vow to do everything in her power to sabotage any Nazi plan she could uncover.

Unwittingly, she and Doug had stumbled onto something. Anna was curious to find out what this ship was carrying. Going below deck she managed to gain access to the forward hold. She opened a large metal door and entered.

At first glance, the contents seemed innocent enough: fifty-five-gallon drums and numerous crates of various sizes on pallets. But there was something curious about the drums that attracted her attention. She moved closer and could see they were from the Norsk Hydro plant at Vemork. She knew this was important and managed to loosen the large hex bolt sealing the top of one of the drums. Perhaps Doug would know more.

Anna examined the contents with intense curiosity. She waved her hand over the opening to push any vapors toward her nose, but there was no odor. Anna looked around the floor of the hold and found a small piece of broken pallet and inserted it into the opening in the top of the drum. The stick came out wet. Anna carefully rubbed the liquid between her fingers to check its viscosity.

Finally, she dabbed her finger on her tongue. There was no taste. It was just water...or was it? Suddenly, she remembered her fellow scientists talking about the Norsk Hydro Plant at Vemork producing 'heavy water,' an essential product for any atomic-bomb project.

Just then, she heard voices as the door to the hold opened and two burly crew members entered. Anna ducked behind some crates to hide while the crewmen scanned the hold with their flashlights. Holding her breath, she overheard them talking.

"She won't be in here; let's go," said the one crew member. The crewmen were looking for her, but they did not really believe she was in the hold, so their search was halfhearted at best. After another quick scan with their flashlights, they left.

Anna let out a sigh of relief and waited a few more minutes. Then she rapidly made her way back to the main deck. She allowed herself to be found on deck, leaning against the railing and looking east at the sliver of light that would soon announce the dawn.

"There! There she is over there," announced one of the officers pointing at Anna. He promptly escorted Anna back to the cabin to rejoin Doug, instructing the guard to keep a close watch on them.

Anna quickly told Doug all she had seen and heard. Certainly, the captain's conversation confirmed that he could not be trusted. More alarming, he probably now knew who they really were and that they were urgently being sought by the Germans. Since it was likely that there would be a reward for their capture, and since Captain Hans was significantly influenced by money, they were now in even greater danger than before.

Doug realized Anna just might be right about the Nazis being responsible for Britta's death. Vowing to help her any way he could, he proceeded to caution her about the seriousness of the situation in which they currently found themselves.

"They will definitely arrest us the minute we get to Rostock." Doug added, "Let's check it out and see if there is a way to get out of here; we can't stay on here and we can't swim. Distracting them somehow to get one of the lifeboats is the only thing I can think of right now."

"Doug, it's liquid from Vemork," said Anna sitting on the bunk.

Doug answered pacing the floor,

"'Heavy water?' For deuterium? Since this ship is headed for Germany, it is probably loaded with supplies for the Nazi war machine, and with more than just Swedish iron ore. I believe that the drums you saw in the hold are filled with 'heavy water,' a necessary ingredient in the processing of uranium to obtain plutonium."

"What can we do?" asked Anna, pacing the floor of the cabin.

Doug replied,

"I want to check out the drums. I should be able to identify exactly what they are." He was one of a very few Americans who knew of Roosevelt's atomic bomb program in the United States. First, they had to get past the crewman who was standing outside their cabin. Doug opened the door suddenly, and before the hapless guard could react, with the butt of his gun he knocked the man out cold and dragged him into the cabin. He quickly bound, gagged and tied him to the bunk.

Doug and Anna made their way to the forward hold where Anna showed Doug the fifty-five-gallon drums containing the 'heavy water.' Doug looked sharply at the crates. The writing was in Swedish, a language Doug could not read well, but he recognized the name Bofors, the great Swedish arms manufacturer.

Doug looked around and found a metal pry-bar which he used to open a long, rectangular crate where he discovered the barrel of a large artillery piece. Another crate revealed the shells for the weapons, while a third crate was full of sacks of cordite powder, the charge used to propel the shell from the gun.

"Doug, we need to get out of here." Anna wanted to leave the hold quickly. She surmised that the crew would soon realize Doug and Anna had left their cabin and might find the crewman Doug had disabled.

Doug said,

"Anna, I do not think this shipment of 'heavy water,' weapons and ammunition should reach Germany under any circumstances."

He started making an improvised fuse to detonate the crates of cordite. With some luck this would cause a huge explosion to cover their escape from the ship. Doug broke off a long piece of wood from a pallet and coated it with some grease and oil that had been spilled on the floor of the hold. He took one end of the wood and placed several sacks of cordite over it. With a small box of matches Doug had in his pocket from the lantern in the cabin, he lit the other end of the wood.

Anna asked, "What are you doing?"

"This is cordite powder. I'm making a fuse. If we detonate these crates, we can make our escape."

Immediately, they ran from the hold and up onto the main deck. Doug still had the metal pry-bar; it would come in handy if they encountered any of *The Wesser*'s crew. Anna and Doug ran to the life raft attached to the side of the aft pilothouse. This raft was specifically designed to detach and float away if the ship sank so fast that the crew had no time to lower a lifeboat from one of the davits.

They loosened the raft and slid it into the cold, choppy Baltic Sea. They jumped overboard and landed inside it. Already *The Wesser* had steamed on, leaving the raft with its two passengers behind.

At the same time a crewman, who had witnessed the two figures running along the deck and jumping overboard, managed to enter the bridge and inform the captain. "Captain, two people have been running to the raft and are jumping overboard."

Captain Hans ordered,

"Get a message to Rostock, now! I was right about those two!"

He grabbed his revolver, the veins in his neck pulsing with anger. However, just as the captain reached the exit to the bridge, a massive explosion blew through the forward hatch. A huge fireball rose above the ship and secondary explosions followed.

Doug pulled Anna down swiftly into the bottom of the raft when the first explosion occurred. They watched as *The Wesser*, her bottom blown out, quickly filled with water. The secondary explosions caused the engineering spaces to flood, and the ship sank in a matter of moments. Doug could spot no survivors in the water. Beams of wood from the wreckage littered the sea around them in all directions as the morning light slowly dawned.

Together, Doug and Anna embraced to stay warm from the frigid Baltic waters. They were both relieved to have made a successful miniscule attack against the Germans and to have survived. Because of their efforts, fewer munitions would reach German shores. And the loss of the 'heavy water' *The Wesser* was carrying would be a significant and expensive loss to the Germans.

35

Rostock Sunrise
April 10th

It was now sunrise and Doug clearly saw the coast of Germany and the harbor of Warnemünde, a city a few miles northeast of Rostock.

"Where are we?" asked Anna.

Doug looked out across the water.

"Definitely Germany, probably Warnemünde." They started paddling the raft toward shore. Boats could now be seen starting out from the harbor toward the column of smoke that marked *The Wesser*'s grave.

"The last thing we want," Doug said, "is to be picked up by the Germans while still in the vicinity of the wreck." As an American, he was neutral, but if Germany could prove he had any part in the demise of *The Wesser*, a serious diplomatic crisis would result. In addition, if any of the crew survived and revealed that Doug and Anna had escaped into the life raft before the explosion, the Germans would be in hot pursuit with a clear idea of their likely onshore landing point.

As they approached shore, the long shore current carried them away from the path of the rescue vessels, allowing them to land on a desolate part of the beach. Doug and Anna quickly made their way over the dunes and away from the beach before their raft was discovered.

Skirting to the west of Rostock, they came across an east-west railroad line. The line was very busy with many trains carrying passengers and freight of all varieties moving along the line. Doug saw that because there was only one track in use; there was a siding and the westbound trains were taking the siding to allow the eastbound trains to pass. Hidden inside a broken shack on the side of the tracks, they watched as the trains rumbled by.

♦ ♦ ♦ ♦ ♦ ♦ ♦ ♦ ♦ ♦

36

Day

April 10th

Another westbound train slowed and took the siding. Doug smiled as he wiped a smudge of dirt off her nose. "Come on," he said as he pulled her to her feet, giving her a quick kiss. "I think boarding now would be our best shot."

Anna nodded and agreed,

"Yes, if it becomes known that we survived and made it to shore, we are valuable prey. We already know the information was transmitted from the freighter that we were onboard."

As a patrol passed by their hiding spot, they thought they had escaped detection. Doug quickly pulled Anna down into a corner with him when a lone soldier, thinking he detected some movement inside, returned and peered through the grimy window. Satisfied that all was quiet inside, he moved on.

This particular train looked like a troop train, but several cars at the rear of the train appeared to be freight cars. As they moved to the rear of the train, they realized that the last cars contained troop horses. Doug managed to pry open one of the doors to the car and they climbed in, moving quietly behind the horses. They hid in the loose hay behind the swinging hayrack.

Just as soon as they had hidden themselves under the hay, a patrol came along the side of the train. Doug looked at Anna and pressed his finger to his lip as he covered her in more hay. The horses in their carriage were agitated by the presence of

Doug and Anna, strangers, in their car. They also could not latch the carriage door from the inside, and this drew the attention of the patrol.

The door opened and a German guard looked in the car, examining the latch to determine if the open door was accidental or deliberate. His presence caused the horses to become even more agitated so they stamped and shuffled around in the car. They could smell his uneasiness.

The guard, not being very fond of such animals in the first place, wrinkled his nose in disgust at the strong smell of manure and ammonia. He quickly withdrew from the car and locked the door securely after him.

Doug pushed some of the hay aside and looked through the gap between the slats of wood.

"Well, Anna, the good news is that he's gone. The bad news is that we are now trapped inside. The bastard locked the door."

A few minutes later, the train slowly entered the main line and began to move westward. Doug tried to open the door but could not. The guard had been careful when he secured it.

"Anna, there are gaps between the slats of wood. If I can loosen a plank next to the car door, I might be able to unlock it."

He was successful in loosening two of the planks and was able to stick his arm through the enlarged gap that he had created to unlatch the door to the car. No longer trapped, he exhaled with a sigh of relief and said,

"That should do it." *Hopefully, the fly that Cunningham gave him was working,* he thought. He settled his lean frame back down next to Anna and hugged her.

37

Train to Münster, Germany
April 10th/11th

Using the hay bales as a bed, they watched the progression of cities—Wismar, Lübeck and Hamburg—as the train moved west. Anna slept in Doug's arms, knowing that they would be running again soon enough. At each station, the train stopped and guards moved along the train checking the cars, but Doug had replaced the latch on the door and placed the slats back into their original position. With no visible disturbance of the routine, they were left undisturbed in the car, although they were careful to hide, just in case, each time the train slowed to a stop.

Both were extremely hungry, but it was too dangerous to forage for food; it had been hours since they had eaten anything. Their last sustenance had only been a hot cup of coffee, compliments of the now-deceased crew of *The Wesser*. Thirst finally drove them to share the water trough with the horses. Doug leaned back against a bale of hay with Anna asleep in his arms under an old horse blanket with the 1st Kavallerie insignia. His thoughts turned once again toward the train and its contents—and the looming threat of war. He realized that this troop movement must be a beginning of the buildup for an invasion of The Low Countries—Holland and Belgium.

At dawn, the train stopped at a siding in Bremen. Doug and Anna could hear the Germans talking outside as they discussed what would happen next. Doug put his ear up against the door to listen.

"Anna, it sounds like the train will be switching lines and heading to Münster, its final destination, arriving by early evening. There the train will stop. The troops and horses will disembark. We do not have many stops left. We will have to get off soon."

◆ ◆ ◆ ◆ ◆ ◆ ◆ ◆ ◆ ◆

38

Train Ride through Germany
April 11th

Doug and Anna spent several hours trying to remember which cities they would pass through, so they could disembark as close to Münster as possible. They decided to jump off just southeast of Osnabrück. The train had been traveling at thirty miles per hour and a jump at that speed would be very risky. If either of them were injured or, even worse, if they broke a limb, escape would become even more difficult. In daylight, they might be seen from the train or by anyone nearby who was looking in the right direction. The train passed through Osnabrück without slowing down and continued on.

Doug pulled aside the loosened boards and opened the carriage door just a bit. They waited until the train slowed down and was passing through an unpopulated area. However, the jump would be too dangerous from here as it was all jagged, rocky countryside. As they moved southwest from Osnabrück, the countryside became more rural, but the train picked up its speed.

Anna became concerned.

"What if the train continues at this pace all the way to Münster?"

Doug reassured her.

"We'll take our chances. It has to slow down at some point."

Finally, the train entered the Eutoburg Wald. Doug opened the door slightly and saw that the train was slowing down to take a curve.

"This jump is going to be risky, but it's all grass on the downhill slopes. They will definitely shoot us if they find us. We have to go now."

Anna looked at him with apprehension.

"That's not very comforting."

The door to their car opened onto the outside of the curve, minimizing the chances that they would be seen when they jumped.

"Anna, be sure to roll when you hit the ground to lessen the shock of the landing."

Anna went first at Doug's urging with Doug following a moment after. He felt that his specialized military training had better prepared him for such a jump, even if the train sped up slightly after Anna made her jump.

Once on solid ground, Doug looked at Anna.

"Anything broken?"

"I don't think so, just a few scratches. Did they see us?"

"No. Come on, we need better cover," replied Doug. They got up, bruised and cut after rolling down the embankment, but they were otherwise fine.

They made their way westward through the forest using the sun as a compass. Their clothes were ragged and worn after being at sea and smelled from their days in the train car with the horses. They heard the gurgling of a stream and quickly ran over to it to take a drink.

As they approached a small stream, Doug laughed.

"A dip in a stream will make us less pungent so we can no longer be located by smell from downwind."

Anna rolled her eyes at his attempt to be silly, no matter how true it might be. They cupped their hands and took a drink from the stream, washed their faces and then quickly walked until they hit the edge of the woods. The sign in front of them read 'Teckenburg'. The village was a few kilometers ahead.

They were cautious as they approached the village. Doug sniffed the air.

"Anna, it smells of freshly baked bread and pies!"

It amplified their pangs of hunger. Doug saw a pie cooling on a windowsill of a small farmhouse on the outskirts of a village.

He looked at Anna.

"Is it worth being caught for a pie?"

Anna replied, "It smells so good, I can't take it."

Doug looked at her again.

"It's better than dying of starvation. Hide behind that wall and I'll meet you there."

Nobody was around to see them, and Doug managed to pilfer the dish. Famished, they hid behind the wall and within minutes devoured the entire blackberry pie. He also snatched up a cap he saw lying on the porch steps. He took it and put it in his pocket.

"Here, put all that blonde hair up," as he handed her the boy's cap. Fortified with food, they discussed how to get out of German-occupied territory as quickly as possible.

Anna looked at him. "So now what?"

"Well, we need to find a way to move more quickly towards the Dutch border. We're sitting ducks on foot."

While they were talking, Doug noticed a motorcycle lean-ing against an outbuilding. Quickly telling Anna to run over and hide in the adjacent woods, he made his way over to the bike. He quietly walked the cycle back into the woods where Anna was crouched down, waiting, her hair up in the stolen boy's cap.

Fortunately, on the ship, one of the smaller crewmen had loaned Anna a change of clothes, and she had been wearing them when they leapt into the life raft of *The Wesser*. Trying to cross the country pretending to be two men instead of a man and a woman would be much safer for them, especially when the Nazis were seeking a couple. It took a few minutes, but Doug was able to hot-wire the bike, and they rode off westward along a secondary road.

39

Dutch Border
April 11th

Doug and Anna traveled by motorcycle cross-country continuing west. A gust of wind had scattered the clouds, and they were grateful for the warmth of the sun.

"How much farther do we have to go?" Anna asked.

"Not far. I figure we are a few miles from the Dutch border and freedom." They rode across a field toward a row of hedges. Suddenly through the break in the brush, they saw a line of trucks.

"A convoy of German military vehicles," Doug yelled over the noise of the machine. Doug cut the engine, and they ditched the cycle in the field and hid until the convoy passed. "From this point on, we are on foot. There will be roadblocks ahead for sure."

After a few more miles of fields and hedgerows, they came across a small brook that led into a canal running east-west. "We will follow the stream as far as we can," Doug said as he grabbed Anna's hand.

By now, it was night again, as they followed the canal to the German-Dutch border bridge that was heavily guarded. German border guards could be heard laughing and drinking. "We have two choices," Doug said matter-of-factly. "We can talk our way across the border without any papers or we can swim."

"Water? Again? Doug, I have had enough for a lifetime!" Anna replied in a discouraged tone.

"So we talk to the Germans?" queried Doug. Anna turned and gave Doug a discouraging look. Doug took her by the hand as his voice softened. "Anna, we are almost there. Hang in there a little longer."

They entered the cold water of the canal and began to carefully wade toward the bridge and the Dutch border.

Suddenly a voice called out "HALT!" Anna and Doug dove into the water as several shots rang out. Shots churned up the water around them, but the guard's aim was poor after a night of drinking. Swimming under water, they managed to cross the border.

Doug whispered,

"We are free," as he hugged Anna.

"Now let's hurry. We need to get as far away from the border as possible."

40

O'Grady's Stable in Brussels
April 12th

Again, Doug and Anna were wet and cold, but they continued for as long as they could, knowing the farther they got from the German border, the better. Hitching a ride with a Dutch farmer they quickly arrived at the Dutch city of Enschede, Doug purchased two train tickets for Brussels and phoned O'Grady whom he expected to find at his thoroughbred stable in Brussels.

O'Grady picked them up at the remote train station of Waterloo on the outskirts of Brussels. He was extremely relieved to see them safe, but simultaneously shocked by their disheveled appearance.

"Good Lord, lad, what happened to you?"

Doug gave O'Grady an abbreviated version of their escape, starting with Britta's death.

"Having discovered Britta murdered in her home, we fled Copenhagen as it was being invaded. A freighter capsized the fishing vessel we were on, and another one that turned out to be carrying weapons and other supplies for the German war effort picked us up. A spark somehow ignited the barrels, and we were fortunate enough to escape in the ship's life raft. We then hid in a German train with horses.

"It's a long story. I'm exhausted. I have been observing German troop movements as we traveled across Germany. I

181

think you were right, my friend, about a war with The Netherlands. We need to get the news to Dumas, Alistair and Washington as quickly as possible."

O'Grady responded.

"We can do this from my communications setup at the stables as soon as we get back there. By the way, your pal Lenny sent a message saying 'Sir Galahad's Sire won the Kentucky Derby.'"

The Derby had not yet taken place. This was Lenny's coded way of letting them know he had arrived safely in the US. O'Grady mentioned that he suspected he had managed to make his way out of Copenhagen by flying to Paris with the help of the embassy attaché in Copenhagen.

Until now, nobody knew if Anna and Doug had even survived.

"I have been getting scores of messages inquiring about you from England—someone high up in the SOE, I think, seeking to determine your whereabouts and whether you got out safely. A dark horse you are, Doug…with friends in high places," O'Grady said, grinning.

Doug was actually relieved to hear this, as it meant Cunningham and Alistair were probably safe. He remembered that Cunningham said the tracking fly did not work in water.

At the stables, Doug sent a coded message to Washington with all that he had learned about the troop concentrations along the western front. He also relayed information about the shipment of 'heavy water' from Norway to Rostock, Germany. Doug was careful not to make any mention of the freighter, *The Wesser*. In his training, the vital importance of deniability was stressed as critical, and on a mission such as this one with America still neutral in the European conflict, it was doubly vital that nobody in Europe know of his part in blowing up the ship.

Helping O'Grady feed the horses was the young boy, Sean, who ran out to hug Doug. He had healed well from his injury with only a small scar to show for it. The man and boy compared their scars.

"You are a brave young man, Sean. I am proud of you," Doug said, placing a steady hand on Sean's shoulder.

Sean smiled the pride clear on his face.

"Thank you, sir. I have been reading books about airplanes. May I ask you some questions?" Then the boy proceeded to pepper Doug with questions about the specifications of different models.

Doug remembered what Dumas had told him about Sean's part in essential information gathering around the stables as the thoroughbreds traveled to their races.

"He has done nothing but talk and ask questions about you since your last visit," O'Grady confided.

"I think Sean has pressed me to hear every story about you that I know from all our years of friendship. I'm glad you are now here to take up the slack and tell him yourself."

As the four of them walked back to O'Grady's main house, Doug introduced Anna to Sean. She was quite taken with the boy. Doug related how Sean had been orphaned and adopted by the O'Grady's. Anna remembered that Doug had lost his parents very early in his life, too.

Ah, you are so good with him, she mused. *It bodes well for the family I hope we will have together once this war is over.* It was clear Sean looked up to Doug as well as O'Grady as an important male influence. *The beginning of a relationship that will last a lifetime,* contemplated the very astute Anna.

41

Brussels

April 12th

Kathleen opened the door and greeted Anna and Doug with a big hug.

"And who is this?" asked Kathleen, smiling.

"This is Anna, Kathleen. We met in Copenhagen and escaped together."

Kathleen, regarding Anna's appearance, said,

"Oh, look at you, poor thing. You must be starving. Let me show you upstairs where you can get cleaned up. I have some clean clothes for you."

Anna gratefully followed Kathleen upstairs, who proceeded to draw a steaming bath laced with lavender oil. She also put out a soft, warm robe on the four-poster antique bed covered by a goose down comforter. Lighting the fireplace in the bedroom, Kathleen turned to leave, to give Anna some privacy and prepare some food for them. Her eye caught Anna removing the five-pointed pentacle hanging from her neck, the ruble now in Anna's pocket.

"Anna, your necklace is beautiful. Did you know that the Celts believed the pentacle was the sign of the Goddess? The pentacle has the point at the top symbolizing feminine energy."

Anna replied,

"Thanks, Kathleen. It was my mother's necklace, but I always thought, until recently, that it was the Star of David. With times as they are, I have been concealing it under my clothing for safety's sake."

Kathleen responded,

"That is probably wise even though it is not actually a Star of David. The concept of the five points was that Ireland had five great roads, five providences and five paths of the law. The circle around the star represents the goddess of the moon. It refracts and reflects all light, bringing the wearer total intelligence, universal wisdom and protection."

Anna sighed,

"Kathleen, after all we have been through, I think it worked." She regarded Kathleen curiously. "My mother kept a medicinal notebook that had a pentacle diagram, a circle around a star just like my necklace, at the top of each page."

Kathleen responded. "I do know that the origins of the pentacle go back to the most remote historical times, as far back as pre-Babylonian history."

"My mother," Anna continued, "told me stories of her ancestors who believed in the power of the moon when reflected upon bright, shimmering water. Apparently, water exposed to the light of the full moon was presumed to be magical. Moon water was gathered for use in healing and childbirth, and sometimes sick children were laid out in the light of the full moon to cure disease."

Kathleen pondered this for a moment.

"You know, this makes sense. The moon has the gravitational power to pull the tides in and out. As our bodies are made up mostly of water, the moon should also have some effect on our human circulatory system. Tides are created because the earth and moon are attracted to one another by magnetic pull, so in the same way, the moon's energy affects all liquid on the earth."

Anna nodded in agreement.

"I remember sitting for hours with my sister, Britta, under the full moon rocking her to sleep."

"In Ireland we believe in those folklores as well as natural remedies made from local bark, roots and herbs. There are people that travel all over the world, especially to the Amazon, to gather bark and herbs from these remote places for medicinal purposes."

Anna was now excited as she was well aware of how her molecular theory played into this.

"I can still picture my mother at the kitchen table, stirring a pot over the fire containing a mixture of mud and herbs found near an old oak tree combined with the sulphur water from a local spring."

"So where did you grow up?"

"I grew up in a small town in Russia, but left for England when I was sixteen." Anna continued, "My mother would add turmeric extract from the rhizome of curcina longo plants along with milk thistle from the silybum marianum plants with sulphur water. This mudpack, applied to a bruise, a cut or to the chest of someone suffering from a bronchial spasm, had amazing curative powers. It could cure a cut knee in an instant and always helped my sister."

"Those are remedies that are passed down from generation to generation. I hope you kept her notebook! Are you familiar with the pagan ritual of bathing in a sulphur spring under moonlight and then standing inside a pentacle drawn in the dirt or sand?"

"Somewhat," said Anna startled.

"As a child I witnessed such a ceremony, although at the time I did not know what it was."

Kathleen continued, "The Pagan Legend says that The Goddess of the Moon will restore youthfulness and health if you bathe in the hot sulphur spring under a full moon."

"Right now a hot bath and some sleep will restore my youthfulness!" said Anna, grinning with a big yawn.

Laughing, Kathleen gave her a big hug. As she turned to leave, she said, "I am so glad you and Doug are all right. Relax, take your hot bath and come downstairs when you are ready. I'm going to prepare some food. I know Doug is starving. Men always are, and you both have been through quite an ordeal, so you must be hungry, too."

"I am, Kathleen. Thank you so much for your kindness and hospitality, but I really need a bath and some sleep!"

"All right," Kathleen agreed, "but I will have something ready for you when you wake up, whether or not it is mealtime. And anyone will tell you I am a VERY good cook." She chuckled as she turned to leave the room.

"Just have a look at O'Grady's belly. Oh, and I'm sure you have noticed that Doug is like family to us, so I am very glad to have you here. It is no trouble at all."

Anna smiled sadly, remembering all the trouble in her wake and Britta's brutal murder in Copenhagen. *Oh, Kathleen, I hope you never have to know how much trouble I can be.* She removed her boy's cap and shook her long hair loose, stepping out of the filthy clothes she had been living in. She soaked in the lavender-scented bath for almost an hour until she finally felt her sore and aching muscles start to relax.

Anna dried herself off with a large towel and put on the robe Kathleen had left for her. She sat by the fireplace drying and combing out her long hair now clean from the chamomile and spearmint shampoo. *I never knew it could feel so luxurious to simply be clean before.*

Now that she was no longer in danger, Anna realized she was exhausted to her bones. She glanced at the necklace on the night table. *I am too tired to think anymore about it, although I must remember at some point to get my mother's notebook back from Dr. Cunningham,* as she yawned. Overcome with drowsiness, she crawled under the down comforter on the large four-poster bed and fell fast asleep.

♦ ♦ ♦ ♦ ♦ ♦ ♦ ♦ ♦ ♦

Meanwhile, Doug had used O'Grady's shower and had shaved, coming down to the kitchen in an oversized white shirt of O'Grady's, a pair of pants a bit too large and thick woolen socks. He devoured more of Kathleen's famous gruel and ale.

O'Grady laughed.

"Well, that's much better—you look human again!"

Doug responded,

"Thanks, I feel like a million bucks." Doug placed his mug on the table, looking at O'Grady.

"I hate to eat and run, but right now I feel like I could pass out on the table," as he stood up.

O'Grady chuckled,

"On with you now. Upstairs to the guestroom. Have a good sleep, and we'll talk again tomorrow."

As Doug's eyes started to close from exhaustion, he excused himself to go upstairs to the O'Grady guestroom to sleep. As he entered the room, warm from the crackling logs in the fireplace, he looked over at Anna fast asleep. He found himself overcome by how beautiful and peaceful she looked. He crawled into bed and fell instantly asleep with his arms around her.

♦ ♦ ♦ ♦ ♦ ♦ ♦ ♦ ♦ ♦

The following evening as the men walked around the stables before dinner, O'Grady confided in Doug.

"I am not happy with the recent developments concerning Mussolini. Churchill will probably become Prime Minister and most of the Royal families have fled to England for safety. Belgium is vulnerable as is The Netherlands and Luxembourg. I believe something is going to happen sooner rather than later.

You and Anna need to get out quickly. The L'Arc de Triomphe thoroughbred race is cancelled again this year."

More importantly, O'Grady was supposed to get German aviation information out using one of the mares going there. Increased German aggression would make it more dangerous than ever. Clearly, the stakes in the world were going up.

O'Grady turned to Doug.

"We will be returning to Shannon tomorrow night with most of the horses as a precautionary measure. I don't know how much longer my identity will remain secure. Only one mare will go on to the stables in Paris under the pretense that she is for sale. We will get someone we trust to obtain and pass on the information concealed inside the horse."

Doug nodded.

"I agree; it's a smart move for you to go back. I promised Anna a few days in Paris together although I would rather that she would come to London, but she has her heart set on this. I will also introduce Anna to Dumas when we get to Paris. Should Dumas agree, I will show her the safe house Lenny and I set up at the beginning of April. I must return to the States to report and get Anna immigration papers. Dumas should be able to protect her in the event that the Germans break through the Maginot Line. Please keep your ears open for news of the continued Nazi search for scientists, as I firmly believe Anna is in more danger than she realizes."

O'Grady nodded in agreement.

42

<u>Departure from Brussels</u>
<u>April 14th</u>

Grateful for the long sleep, hot bathes and comforting food, Anna and Doug departed for Paris having enjoyed the rest and warm hospitality of the O'Gradys. Anna gave Kathleen a big hug goodbye, kissed O'Grady on the cheek and ruffled Sean's hair, thanking them both.

Doug shook hands with the man and boy and kissed Kathleen on the cheek, saying,

"Until next time. Thank you so much for everything."

♦ ♦ ♦ ♦ ♦ ♦ ♦ ♦ ♦

Anna felt very pretty in Kathleen's blue cotton dress. She climbed with Doug into O'Grady's truck. Sean and a stable hand hopped in the back for the short ride to the Brussels train station. The station was full of people struggling with their luggage upon arriving and departing the station to and from all destinations in Europe.

"Doug, we'll let our stable hand purchase the tickets for you, just in case any Secret Police are watching the station," said O'Grady as they parked in front of the station.

"I agree," replied Doug.

The stable hand returned with two tickets to Paris. O'Grady took the tickets and handed them to Doug.

"Take care, my friend."

191

O'Grady waved as he watched Anna and Doug dissolve into the crowd. He was about to leave, but he decided to stick around for a few minutes and told Sean to stay in the truck. As always, having worked with horses for so long, his intuition told him something was not right.

Doug and Anna waited in a quiet corner of the station with their tickets as they looked up at the train board. The Paris train was to depart in five minutes. Doug looked out toward the platform. His senses went on full alert upon seeing Lukas and Finn.

"Anna, don't look now, but standing in our way are the same two thugs that Lenny and I fought with at the nightclub in Copenhagen. They are Sicherheitsdienst and deadly assassins. Apparently, Alistair was right when he said we are on their 'hit list.' I should stay here and distract them while you get on the train to Paris."

Anna shook her head adamantly.

"No. I will stay with you, Doug."

Lukas and Finn stood attentively by the entrance to the train platforms. Lukas finished his cigarette and stamped it out. Finn adjusted his jacket, barely concealing his revolver. They eyeballed each passenger as they came onto or left the platform.

Anna looked at the train board and quickly tugged at Doug's sleeve.

"Doug, I have an idea. Look at the train board. There's a train leaving for Amsterdam on the track next to ours, and it is due to leave just a few minutes before our train for Paris."

"Anna, that's a great idea!" Doug looked proudly at her.

They boarded the Amsterdam train with Finn and Lukas trailing behind them.

"Anna, run toward the back end of the car and open the emergency door."

As the train began to move Doug upset some luggage, and they jumped off before the train had cleared the platform. By the time Lukas and Finn managed to get through the upset luggage and jump off the train, Doug and Anna had already boarded the Paris train which had closed its doors and was pulling out of the station.

Finn and Lukas were too late to catch the train. They had missed their target, once again. Running outside, the two jumped into a dusty gray car. Sean had been watching the whole scene from the driver's seat having a clear view into the station. He put the truck into gear and plowed after them, pushing their car off the road and into a ditch. O'Grady ran outside just in time to see Sean taking off after the men in his truck.

"Jesus, Mary and Joseph, what is that child getting himself into? I never should have shown him how to drive the truck around the stables," O'Grady muttered angrily.

Sean drove the truck right back with a big grin on his face and proudly declared,

"Dad, I pushed them off the road into a ditch; their car is wrecked. If they were trying to follow the train with Anna and Doug, they won't be able to now."

O'Grady gave in with a smile and ruffled Sean's hair, saying,

"Move over, I'm driving. Son, you want to be very careful. Those men are trained killers. I'll be glad to get you back to Ireland."

Sean grinned the whole way back to the stables.

◆　◆　◆　◆　◆　◆　◆　◆　◆　◆

On the train to Paris, Doug turned to Anna, his expression serious.

"Anna, I am going to introduce you to a Parisian gentleman by the name of Dumas. He will see you safely to a secure location, if necessary, while I am gone. I hope to actually show you the house Dumas has secured for our use, if the need arises. By now those two Sicherheitsdienst thugs will know we are headed to Paris. You must promise me to be very careful and never go out alone once I leave for the States and if things get worse get to Dumas or Dr. Cunningham in London right away."

Anna looked quietly at Doug.

"I'll be fine. Margo is in Paris, and I can look her up. Besides, after all we've gone through, staying in and reading a good book sounds positively delightful."

They would have too few romantic days and nights together in Paris, known as the world's most beautiful city for lovers.

♦　♦　♦　♦　♦　♦　♦　♦　♦　♦

43

Trip to Paris
April 16th

Doug and Anna arrived in Paris safely, where they checked into a small hotel-apartment. For the next several days, they enjoyed the sights of Paris by day and spent their nights together in the apartment that Doug had rented for a few months. Their love for each other grew deeper with each passing hour.

Evenings, they explored the cafés of Montmartre and took in the shows. Doug delighted in Anna's excitement and laughter.

"I forget sometimes," he teased, "how many years you spent looking into a microscope and calculating mathematical sequences and equations."

Anna looked down and blushed, hiding her face with the swing of her hair. They continued walking, hand in hand.

One day, Doug drove her out to the country, and he pointed out the chateau—their safe house—to her.

"Anna, if there is ever an emergency, contact my friend Dumas. He will bring you to this location and clear you past the nuns. You can come here and be safe."

"Who is Dumas?" inquired Anna.

"You can trust Dumas; he works with us," Doug asserted.

"And if he contacts you, please go with him immediately. He has access to information not available to less informed civilians."

Anna looked at him seriously.

"Hopefully that won't be necessary, but I will do whatever you say."

On their last evening together, Doug took Anna to Harry's Bar and told her that he wanted to go over the plans he had in mind for their future. After they ordered their dinner and drinks, Doug's demeanor became serious.

He looked deeply into Anna's eyes, hypnotizing her with their intensity. "Anna," he began, "you know of my work. I am always on call for my government. If the war escalates—especially if the United States joins in—who knows how long it will be before I am able to switch over to a corporate career." He stopped to let the gravity of his statement sink in.

Anna nodded slowly, a questioning look in her eyes at his solemn tone, but she said nothing. She waited.

Doug took a deep breath, and then plunged ahead.

"Anna, knowing all of this about me and my life, is there any chance that you would give serious consideration to becoming my wife?"

Anna, with a look of pure surprise on her face, answered without hesitation,

"Yes!"

"You will have to wait for a little while. I have to complete my assignment and will return to Paris for you as quickly as I can." Doug needed to pave the way to put the paperwork in place before Anna would be allowed to enter the United States with him. They decided to get married on July 4th in Virginia. Until then, Anna agreed to stay in Paris in the hotel-apartment before returning with Doug to the U.S. in mid-June.

44

Doug in London and Ireland
April 20th

Duty called and Doug was summoned to the States to report directly to the top brass on all that he had learned. Anna and Doug's last moments together were filled with passion, making love with an intensity that left them both shaken to the core. The next morning, Anna kissed Doug goodbye, unable to stop the tears spilling down her cheeks.

"Please don't cry, darling," Doug implored as he hugged her and promised to return in a few weeks for his bride-to-be.

Dumas sat in his car, waiting to drive Doug to the airport. He looked at Doug as he got in the front seat.

"C'est l'amour, mon ami. Don't worry; I will look after her."

♦ ♦ ♦ ♦ ♦ ♦ ♦ ♦ ♦ ♦

Dumas drove him to Le Bourget Airport for the flight to London. Doug had arranged to spend his layover time having lunch with Alistair at The Aristocrat Pub before hopping on the plane to Shannon for the last leg of the journey back to the United States.

As Doug entered the pub, Alistair promptly stood up.

"Good to see you, old chap! Glad you made it out in one piece," as he enthusiastically shook Doug's hand.

Doug smiled at him.

"Likewise, Alistair! How did you and Cunningham escape?"

The men sat down in a private booth and ordered lunch, then exchanged stories.

"After we left you, we managed to board a Dutch tanker eventually meeting up with the British Royal Navy fleet in the Atlantic, weathering treacherous storms to Scotland. It was quite an ordeal, I might add, getting all that gold on. I was afraid the tanker would sink," he grinned in his comical way.

Alistair described his harrowing escape from Copenhagen with the help of Dr. Cunningham.

"We never would have made it without his help."

Doug added, "Watching him work the night of the invasion was very impressive."

Alistair replied, "Yes, he is very good. He was instrumental in our successful escape with the eighty tons of gold coins and bullion. We took it to the vault in The Bank of England for safekeeping without losing a single coin to the Germans, despite a few narrow escapes while in transit."

"That's fantastic! You know, Alistair, if you ever told the public that story, they would never believe you. Sounds a bit like a Hollywood film to me," chuckled Doug.

Alistair, with a resounding laugh, replied,

"Cheers!" as he took a big gulp of his gin and tonic.

"Sounds like you've got a bloody good story too, and you got the girl out. More on that in a moment! Actually, it's a bit gloomy and dull now that the excitement is over. Do tell me what you've learned?!" He took out his gold Dunhill lighter to light his Dunhill cigarette.

Doug responded,

"The troops are amassing to take the Low Countries."

Alistair leaned in closer, interested, as Doug described the troop movements he witnessed while traversing Germany.

Alistair exhaled cigarette smoke.

"Bloody Germans. They won't stop now. Now what of these scientist refugees heading for the US? How can we help?"

Doug discussed the necessity of a plan for the escape of scientist refugees to the United States.

"They will need safe passage by land, sea or air, and we need to put some sort of screening process in place and provide the scientists with proper documents and identification. Do you have an apparatus in place to handle that?" Doug inquired. "In a rescue operation like this, no need to tell you, we must be particularly careful not to allow enemy agents across our borders."

After a moment, Alistair quietly said,

"I do have something important to discuss with you."

"What is it Alistair?" inquired Doug.

"The Gestapo apparently learned that Anna escaped to Paris." He showed Doug a copy of the wire they intercepted.

Doug tried not to think about the possible outcomes, but he could not help being amazed at the Nazis' comprehensive intelligence network. Someone had put the puzzle pieces together rather quickly. Every instinct screamed for him to return to Paris immediately and rescue Anna from this danger, but his commitment to his country required that he complete his mission first. He told Alistair of his encounter with Lukas and Finn in Brussels.

Hopefully, he thought, *they do not know where she is staying.* Still, he wanted to get word through Alistair to Dumas to tell Anna to be extra careful.

Doug reviewed the telegram "Shit. This is not good. Will you please get a message to Dumas for me today and ask him to make sure that Anna gets to the chateau immediately?"

Alistair responded "Of course! Are you sure you don't want her to come to London?"

Doug shook his head "She wants to stay in Paris with her friend. Did I tell you I have asked her to marry me?"

Alistair surprised said

"Good God man! That's a big step! My sincere congratulations! Cheers!" as both men clinked glasses

Alistair then sat back his smile turning to a frown.

" Doug, there is something amiss with some communications. That message was sent from an unknown source from the chateau in Paris at the exact time you were there."

Doug slammed his fist on the table

"What do you mean? This is very disturbing. No one knew we were in Paris except O'Grady and Dumas. Alistair, the only communication that I sent was out of Brussels. I did not send any communication from Paris." Doug looked at the telegram in his hand as Alistair said, "That is the copy of the communication in question."

"Alistair, was this sent from the chateau cottage? Obviously you have a special code to identify where a message is being sent from. I did drive Anna by one day but we never went in. I'll have to think about this. What are your thoughts?"

"I'm not sure. I just wanted to inform you. We learned that Lenny made it out through the Embassy, which we believe is compromised! Come, I'll give you a ride to the airport. The boy Sean will be waiting for you at Shannon. We got him on the plane for the ride back to Washington with you."

His first thought was O'Grady. *Could O'Grady be the one compromising the security of communications? I have known him for years,*

Doug rationalized. *Surely I would have sensed something suspicious about him before now. But O'Grady was already back at the stables in Ireland so the timing was off too. Dumas had too much to lose since he needed their help. Cunningham…perhaps he had been unduly harsh with him? Anna? No, she had trusted him with her formula. And Lenny was back in the States.*

Doug decided to chew on the information for a while. On a napkin, he wrote down the date of the communication in question. After all, O'Grady had access to the Germans, and was selling horses in Germany, albeit as an excuse to get information in and out, and had the communication skills to send the messages in the proper format. Doug tried to put this together but decided he would visit with O'Grady when he stopped in Ireland. He would be able to make a more informed decision once he had the opportunity to ask a few pointed questions. His thoughts were soon drawn back to Anna and the danger she was in now.

◆ ◆ ◆ ◆ ◆ ◆ ◆ ◆ ◆ ◆

After lunch, Alistair drove Doug to the airport where he boarded another DC-3 for the first leg of the long flight back to the States. The first part of the flight was a quick stop to Ireland.

In Shannon, O'Grady and Sean greeted Doug at the airport. O'Grady had previously agreed to Doug's plan to help Sean go to school in the United States. O'Grady was traveling so much with the horses and since there was mounting concern over a second world confrontation, Sean's safety had become of paramount concern to them all. In addition, if the Nazis were aware of O'Grady's identity, they might also suspect Sean's role in the information web.

The O'Gradys were unwilling for their adopted son to be endangered if Doug was able to offer a viable alternative. He would attend private school and then go on to boarding school in Massachusetts. Sean was excited about the opportunity of starting school in America.

Sean would return to Ireland to the O'Grady's, in the summers and for holidays. Kathleen was not happy about Sean's imminent absence and was quite vocal about it. However, she did realize the danger that Sean would be in if the German aggression continued. In the way of young boys who had no sense of their own mortality, Sean was increasingly eager to participate in listening to German conversations and passing on the information.

His own dedication to his adopted parents and the cause had led Sean into increasingly daring escapades. He would be safer far away, and while the United States might abandon their neutral status at some point, the war was unlikely to reach that far. Sean clearly possessed a clever mind and leadership qualities. He should be afforded the best education.

♦ ♦ ♦ ♦ ♦ ♦ ♦ ♦ ♦ ♦

Once on the plane, Doug settled back into his window seat. As he stared out the airplane window, he was glad for the downtime to think quietly during the flight back to Washington. He was sure of O'Grady's loyalty, after all he was trusting him with his son.

He was not happy about leaving Anna in Paris, an uneasy premonition spread through him.

45

Trip to Chartres

Margo, Anna's old friend from Copenhagen, was living in Paris, and Anna was able to locate her through her family. Anna knew Margo would be happy to see her and likewise, she was looking forward to seeing her friend. Doug thought the relaxation and shopping would be a good distraction for her since he knew she was still mourning her loss of Britta.

Margo was working for a small designer boutique that introduced a perfume in 1922 called Chanel N°5. Anna rang her up at the shop, and Margo, thrilled to hear from her old friend, came to visit her at the hotel-apartment that afternoon. As the girls caught up, Anna confided in her, describing the scene of Britta's murder and her feelings about it.

"Margo, I know Doug thinks this will be a good distraction for me, but I miss Britta so. When I close my eyes, I can still see that blood and her sprawled body on the floor by the hanging sheets. She was so much healthier that I had begun to hope…and then, in an instant, she was dead. I was prepared for her to die of the lung disease or hemophilia because I watched her ailing for so many years, but this…" Anna suddenly broke down and started to cry.

Margo was horrified by what had happened to Britta.

"Oh, Anna, how I wish you had both come with me and left Copenhagen when I asked you that day," Margo said mournfully.

"Britta would still be alive if you had."

In an effort to distract a brooding Anna who was also upset about Doug's departure, Margo invited Anna to go to the stables with her the next day. The family that owned part of the boutique was also one of the world's leading racehorse owners. Anna was introduced to Pierre Wertheimer, who, along with his brother Paul, were Coco Chanel's partners in the House of Chanel perfume business.

She must have gone to the ladies' room, thought Anna, as she walked around the stables, realizing that Margo had disappeared.

♦ ♦ ♦ ♦ ♦ ♦ ♦ ♦ ♦ ♦

Meanwhile, in one of the back lot stalls, a man extracted German aviation plans from one of the mares. He handed the papers over to Margo who quickly put them in her bag and then slung the large handbag over her shoulder. Buttoning up her Canary yellow jacket, she then turned and hurried back to Anna who was talking with one of the grooms. Margo had made the decision not to tell Anna as she was sworn to secrecy.

♦ ♦ ♦ ♦ ♦ ♦ ♦ ♦ ♦ ♦

Despite the threat of war in other parts of Europe, the nightlife of Paris carried on as before. However, such moments in time passed all too quickly.

Anna and Margo decided to visit the Cathedral at Chartres which was only forty-five minutes from Paris. Margo was determined to keep Anna's spirits up, and Anna was curious to learn more about the magic spring water that ran underneath the Cathedral. She wondered if there were common properties between the water of her childhood sulphur springs and this spring.

Anna and Margo drove to The Cathedral Notre Dame of Chartres and tagged along with an English-speaking tour guide who explained,

"Chartres Cathedral is among the best preserved of the major French cathedrals with an extensive collection of sculpture and stained glass. It was also a major site of pilgrimage in honor of the Virgin Mary to whom the Cathedral is dedicated."

The guide went on earnestly.

"Chartres' history as a holy place has legendary roots in the pre-Christian era when Druids, the Celtic priests of Britain and Gaul, held sacred rites in natural settings like the forest groves and underground grottoes that once lay at Chartres. According to mystical legend, the Druids believed Chartres to be a place where spiritual energy emanated from the earth and they worshipped at its grottoes—now supposedly part of the cathedral's crypt—which were connected to a sacred spring. According to some scholars, the Gauls of that era created statues of protective mother goddesses with infants on their knees which were placed near the sacred waters."

She continued,

"A well underneath the crypt dating from Gallo-Roman times leads to the underground waters believed to have been revered by a secret Pythagorean sect. Pythagorean initiates were required to swear a secret oath by the Tetractys symbol. The five-pointed star, a mystical symbol which symbolized the four elements—earth, air, fire and water—was frequently worn as a dedication of faith. The prayer of the Pythagoreans was:

'Goddess of the moon from the deepest dark of time, let us drink this magical water and under your powerful moonbeams become divine.'

As the guide kept walking she explained, "The Tetractys is a triangular figure consisting of ten points arranged in four rows which add up to the 'perfect number Ten.' It was sometimes called the 'Mystic Tetrad.' The novices swore the oath and then maintained a period of silence for three years. The Tetractys was a secret symbol and the sect recognized each other by a pentacle, a star with five points inside a circle."

Anna's mind was spinning as she remembered her childhood experience near the sulphur spring and the ring of people she saw holding hands and chanting under the full moon. *Now this made sense*, she thought, with the startling revelation that her mother had been a part of the Pythagorean society. That sulphur spring in Russia had obviously been a place of Pythagorean worship. They kept and protected the secret of the spring. Now her mother's necklace and theories of the moon and the natural remedies Anna had read about in her mother's notebook were all making sense. This was connected to her star on the necklace. She thought about her conversation with Kathleen again.

Margo looked at Anna.

"This is actually fascinating. I know that the Tetractys and its mysteries influenced the early kabbalists; a Hebrew Tetractys is similar."

Anna could barely contain her excitement.

"Oh Margo, thank you for bringing me here. I think my mother knew about this!"

Margo pointed,

"Over there! The Labyrinth…let's go check it out!"

Another English-speaking tour guide was showing a different group of tourists the Labyrinth. Again, the girls listened in.

"This Gothic cathedral was a landmark in architectural innovation, relying on columns, pointed arches and flying buttresses rather than walls to carry the weight of the building. This allowed the architects to expand the building upward to more than twice the height of earlier cathedrals and freed the walls to be filled with the now-famous stained-glass windows."

They continued walking, gazing up.

"The design of the church involved 'sacred geometry,' the use of numbers, angles and shapes that mirror the principles the faithful believe that God used in creating the universe. The cathedral's floor is inlaid with a labyrinth, a winding circular pathway that facilitates a walking meditation. The labyrinth symbolized the pilgrimage to Jerusalem which was not feasible for most European Christians. It was also symbolic as life's journey to triumph over evil."

Anna thought about the Pentacle in ancient Greece. Pythagoras was credited with the invention of the Tetractys. The pentacle was a secret sign dating back 2,500 years—and my mother had one. *I would like to talk to Kathleen again about this. And Dr. Cunningham!*

She wondered again if this sacred stream running under the cathedral held the same molecular properties as the one near her home in Russia.

Two rough-looking men had followed the girls into the Cathedral and were now watching Margo and Anna, hidden behind the curving buttress.

"…looking at the labyrinth, which had been laid into the floor around the year 1200."

Anna turned to Margo, eager to share her knowledge, and whispered,

"This is an eleven-circuit design, divided into four quadrants. You are supposed to walk it several times before reaching a goal," she explains. "It has served for centuries as a substitute for an actual pilgrimage to Jerusalem and was called 'The Chemin de Jerusalem.'"

"How do you know all this?" inquired Margo.

"I read something about it in my mother's notebook years ago, although I didn't make much of it at the time." She glanced at the two tourists next to her. They were listening to Anna and Margo's conversation. As she looked over her shoulder, she had that uncanny feeling of being watched. Danger alarms were going off in her head.

"Margo, let's go back now. I'm getting a headache."

Margo looked over at Anna and noticed she was rather pale.

"Of course, but let's stop at my apartment first. I have a headache tonic that will help you feel much better."

With that, both girls walked briskly to Margo's car and drove back to Paris, unaware that Lukas and Finn were following them closely in a dusty, gray van.

♦ ♦ ♦ ♦ ♦ ♦ ♦ ♦ ♦ ♦

Margo's quaint apartment was in the busy Champs-Élysées district. After finding a parking spot right in front, both girls got out of the car and walked into the building as the door attendant tipped his hat as he opened the door for them.

Lukas and Finn watched the girls enter the building from their van.

"Well, at least now we know where one of them lives."

"Right," Finn replied angrily, "but what good does it do us? We cannot follow them in with the doorman standing outside."

"We will watch the apartment over the next few days. If the female scientist lives here, we will find a way in. If she doesn't, sooner or later the other one will lead us to her." Lukas warned Finn,

"Caution Finn. If we're caught, they will try us as Nazi spies. It's time for us to report back to our commanding officer."

They put the van in gear and drove off.

♦ ♦ ♦ ♦ ♦ ♦ ♦ ♦ ♦ ♦

46

Zurich, Hotel Room

In a modest hotel room in Zurich, Switzerland, two men met confidentially. The German nodded quickly and in a thick accent said,

"Per our previous negotiations, we will release the eight Jewish scientists you have requested who are currently held at the labor camp outside of Warsaw. Have you been able to obtain what we want?"

Dr. Cunningham answered,

"It was difficult, but, yes, I have what you want, the penicillin."

"Good. We will release the prisoners to you at the prearranged location on the French-German border the day after tomorrow."

"We will have the penicillin at the exchange point."

Dr. Cunningham rose and reached for the door. He stood there for a moment pondering if he could trust his old colleague from Germany with whom he had worked many years ago.

His next plan would be to work on getting these scientists to Dumas' escape boat which would take them from Barfleur to Southampton, and then to the US. He would need a truck with medical supplies and some of Dumas' armed men.

I will be on the truck myself. These men will need medical attention and food before getting to Barfleur. Cunningham had paid the Resistance for the penicillin with the exchange of weapons and ammunition. *Professor Karl Brandt would need much more than the penicillin I will give him in order for it to work on anyone, including Hitler. Donovan will appreciate my assistance in getting these scientists out; after all, they honored my request to have Doug assigned to this mission. A favor for a favor. At least I know from London headquarters he made it to London. They had been able to track him through Germany to Brussels safely.*

◆ ◆ ◆ ◆ ◆ ◆ ◆ ◆ ◆ ◆

Back in Paris, it was a dark and damp night. Downstairs at a sleazy strip club, a man watched a stripper's body shimmy seductively to the music onstage. *She definitely knows how to seduce an audience,* he thought, licking his lips and remembering the first time he saw her. He would have her in his own way, but not yet; there was business to be taken care of first.

The meeting with the German was taking too long. He looked over at the man whose belly was so large it rested on his thighs. He was now making snide remarks as the shots of vodka went down faster and faster. *Best to get him back to business before he gets too drunk,* he thought.

"How many Reichsmarks for the molecular formula?" he demanded.

◆ ◆ ◆ ◆ ◆ ◆ ◆ ◆ ◆ ◆

Later that night, after the German stumbled out of the club and drove off in a drunken stupor, he watched and waited behind the club for the stripper to come out. He watched her close the back door of the bar behind her. She slid into the passenger seat of his car and handed him a piece of torn notepaper.

"We have a deal, right? I get half of the money?" she asked eagerly.

He looked at the symbols on the scrap of paper. Soon, the formula and money would be all his. The thought of slicing her neck, like he had with the others, excited him. For now, she could spend the night pleasing him. He would plan a future rendezvous with her in an abandoned warehouse, not too far from the French coastline near Cherbourg, in the little town of Barfleur.

47

Paris, Anna's Hotel Apartment

Closing the door to the small, Paris hotel-apartment where she and Doug had shared their all too short time together, Anna walked quickly down the long flight of stairs to the street below. It was the first day in a long time that she had even felt like getting out of bed. Although it was a beautiful, sunny afternoon, she had a scarf tied around her head with sunglasses on. Dumas had warned her to keep a low profile based on Alistair's classified information and Doug's urgent request.

So Anna had been living quietly. Holland and Belgium had surrendered to the Nazis. With Doug gone, she felt in limbo waiting for his return. Other than the occasional walk in the park, and the one trip to Chartres Cathedral, she now kept mostly to herself. Tonight, however, Margo was coming over for dinner in yet another attempt to cheer her up.

Yesterday on a walk in Montmartre, she thought she glimpsed Britta, but lost sight of the figure in the crowd. *I am now imagining things. I saw Britta dead with my own eyes! How long will this sadness continue? I am so tired of being tired.*

Anna held a note in her hand to meet Dumas at a local café close to her apartment. She hoped to hear good news, or for that matter, any news, from Doug preferably giving a date for his return. She tried to keep her spirits up, but every day she felt more and more despondent. Before Doug departed for the States, he had told her to trust Dumas, so she was hopeful

213

that he would have good news for her. *If I even knew what date Doug was coming back, I think I could bear the waiting better,* Anna thought.

Anna arrived early for her meeting with Dumas. She sat quietly at a corner table reading the front page of the newspaper. It seemed the French Stripper Ripper had struck again. In frustration, Anna threw the paper face down on the chair next to her. She could not bear to look at the picture of the bloodied stripper's body. It reminded her too much of Britta.

Shortly, Dumas strode in, all smiles. She was relieved and happy to see him. He greeted her with a friendly kiss on each cheek, and after ordering deux cafés au lait, he began.

"Anna, thanks for coming. As you know, I promised Doug I would look out for you, and I keep my promises. We have learned of certain Gestapo agents snooping around, making inquiries about a female scientist from Copenhagen. You are all too obvious, ma chère, so I must insist that you pack a few belongings and come with me today.

"I must pick up some papers from a friend, but I will be back for you in half an hour. There is a safe house in the country where you can stay for a while until I am able to contact Doug. He will provide us with further instructions on your route and the paperwork needed to get you to safety in the United States."

Anna replied,

"Yes, I understand. Doug said to go with you immediately if there was a problem. Merci, Jacques, but what have you heard from Doug? I have heard nothing for weeks now. He told me it would only be a few weeks, and it has been more, much more. Has something gone wrong?"

Dumas said lowering his voice,

"No, nothing is wrong. I have not had word from him, but patience, Anna. Communication is very difficult right now, and most lines are down or intercepted. Remember, Doug is very aware that you are in danger. He may be reluctant to contact us when he is not sure which communication channels are compromised for fear of leading them straight to you. With Paris likely to be occupied, the French government has moved to Bordeaux.

"France is in trouble, and Italy has also declared war against us. We really should get you out while we can. I am arranging for boat travel for some scientists from one of the smaller ports to go to Southampton. I want to contact Doug first to make sure that traveling by sea will be the safest passage for you. Anna, he is a man of his word. Please trust him…and me…for just a little bit longer."

Anna needed to leave Paris right away. While they discussed their plans, Anna saw a man out of the corner of her eye. She glimpsed him for only a moment, but she swore that it was Dr. Spelman. When she looked a second time, he was gone.

This is the second time; first Britta, then Dr. Spelman—now I am sure I am going crazy. I wonder what ever happened to him?

Anna ran to the hotel-apartment to pack her few belongings. She picked up the phone to call Margo at her apartment to cancel their dinner for this evening, but there was no answer. *Perhaps she is on her way already; I will leave her a note,* thought Anna.

Dumas said that he would retrieve his car and return for her within half an hour. She quickly put her new clothes in an old suitcase and, underneath them, hid the ruble inside the music box. Sitting down on the bed, she pulled out the music box again and opened the lid. The beautiful melody made the tears start to well up in her eyes as she thought of how much had happened since the day in that little jewelry store.

A few minutes later, Anna heard a knock at the door. Quickly, she hid the music box out of sheer instinct putting it inside one of her boots in the suitcase and placed the bag under the mattress. She put the other one on the chain around her neck. *It's surely Dumas but he said half an hour,* she thought *unless it's Margo showing up a bit early.* Nonetheless, she felt better hiding it for the moment.

"Just a minute," she shouted in eager anticipation of Dumas' return. As she opened the door and her heart jumped into her throat when she saw a disheveled Dr. Spelman standing before her. Anna was stunned.

As her hand gripped the door handle, she said cautiously,

"Dr. Spelman, what are you doing here?"

He reacted as if he had not heard anyone call him that in some time. His eyes filled with tears. Reluctantly, Anna invited Dr. Spelman in. She looked up and down the hallway for any sign of Dumas before closing the door.

Dr. Spelman sat himself on the couch, his hand holding his hat on his knee, as he confessed to Anna the entire story: how threats from Nazi officials including Lukas and Finn had turned him into a traitor.

"Don't you understand, Anna? I was afraid for my life. I bet you would have done the same thing in my position…especially if your sister was threatened. Or maybe not.."

He explained how the Nazis wanted the formula as part of the German effort to build a "Super Race." They also saw possibilities for its destructive power in wiping out populations by simple insertion into the water supply, by chemically manipulating it.

Dr. Spelman asked Anna how her sister was doing and if she was in Copenhagen. A lump formed in her throat as the memories flooded back and her eyes filled with tears. Dr. Spelman, upon hearing about her sister's murder, felt responsible for what happened.

"I am so sorry, Anna. I told Lukas and Finn that you had discovered the final component for the formula derived from the sulphur springs water. You did figure it out, right?" he inquired, still not one hundred percent sure.

Anna, who had had time to process the whole sequence of events, simply replied,

"The day I discovered the final bit of the formula was the day I put our entire world at risk. Remember, it only took the idea of one man to burn the library in Alexandria. Perhaps it is not up to us to change the course of humanity, especially if it gets into the wrong hands."

Anna hesitated, instantly regretting what she had said. Doug had warned her to not discuss her discovery with anyone.

Dr. Spelman revealed,

"I was given a sum of money in return for the notebook, the serum and my research. I took it. I figured it would take their scientists some time to figure it out. I left Copenhagen and the Institute for Paris the day before the Germans overran Copenhagen."

He continued,

"Without any knowledge of the invasion, my plan was only to escape the two Sicherheitsdienst agents who were following me and eventually go to the United States." He told Anna that the Nazis already had the bulk of the formula, and the final instructions were all that was stopping them from creating the most powerful molecular formula that the world would ever know.

Commenting on the paradox of the water's nature—that it could save and kill within a few degrees of itself—Anna lied to Dr. Spelman.

"I lost the last part of the instructions for the formula in my travels from Copenhagen, and it is unlikely that anyone who finds it would know what it is." The microfilm was concealed in the ruble around her neck. She would never trust

Dr. Spelman again. Although she did believe he was genuinely sorry for what had happened, Anna knew that he mostly felt sorry for himself.

Finally, he asked what it had felt like when she figured out the formula.

Anna said

"It turned out to be less than I would have ever guessed. At any rate I replaced the serum with tap water."

"You did what? That means they only have regular water. Now they will really want revenge." He wondered aloud if she could remember any of the final bits of the formula. "If we can recreate it, we would have a major bargaining chip with the Nazis as well as all the other governments and companies."

Anna neither wanted to bargain with them nor could she recreate it. *And I wouldn't even if I could. I'm glad I never shared my discovery with him. To think that I once admired him.*

Dr. Spelman begged.

"Anna, consider the future generations of people who could benefit from this, especially in the right hands."

Anna was now running out of patience with him, knowing he would never give up. She asked Dr. Spelman never to discuss the matter with her again. She was putting it behind her, along with Britta's murder.

"But it's so powerful a discovery!"

Anna responded angrily,

"I know the power of it. I've seen it give life, but I also know that it can be deadly if manipulated and so do you, and you were willing to give it to the Germans for your own benefit."

Dr. Spelman handed Anna a letter.

"Please do not open it until you reach America. It is possible that I may not make it over and this is the least I can do to try to make it up to you," he said, assuming that was where she would go.

"I apologize again for my part in your sister's death and for the danger I put you in." He glanced at her hauntingly beautiful eyes again, now cold with anger. *Perhaps she was right,* he thought. *Some experiments should be abandoned before they wreak havoc on this world.*

"Dr. Spelman, please leave now. There is nothing you can do to bring back my sister. We have nothing more to say to each other." She was furious he had put her in such danger. Anna also held him responsible for Britta's death. *I will never forgive him for that.*

Defeated, yet unburdened of his secret betrayal, Dr. Spelman grabbed his coat and put on his hat to leave.

Unbeknownst to him, Lukas had seen him entering Anna's building as they were following Margo to Anna's apartment. Having disposed of Margo, Lukas and Finn had entered the building and were silently waiting and listening off to one side of the apartment door. Furious, now that they heard the formula for which they paid was plain water, they were intent on getting their revenge. Having overheard the conversation that Anna no longer had the formula, they were convinced Spelman knew more than he was admitting to.

As Dr. Spelman started to open the door, it was pushed open with a loud bang. Standing there were two men snarling with malice written all over their faces. Anna recognized them instantly from the train station in Brussels. These men were the Secret assassins from Brussels and the club in Copenhagen. She knew every second was critical now as her heart pounded.

These men killed Britta, she thought angrily.

Finn quickly dug into his pocket and made a quick move toward Anna. She heard a quick snap as the blade smacked into place. She stared at the knife—four inches of curved wickedness.

"Oh, my God," whispered Anna. Quickly she grabbed the closest vase and threw it at him. He easily dodged it. She heard the crash of the vase and then a groan. She quickly turned to see Dr. Spelman bashed in the face by Lukas. The entire sitting room had been overturned. He was struggling to get on his feet, shaking his head the way a dog would, while wiping the blood from his mouth.

Finn ran toward Anna with the blade glinting as he swiped at her for the kill. With total rage, Anna grabbed the fireplace poker and swung at the man, unmindful of the knife.

"Bitch," he snarled as he grabbed the instrument away from her. He was immensely strong, and with great force, he slammed into her, pitching her head first into the glass coffee table, the intensity of the force shattering the table in a shower of glass fragments.

She felt her head explode with white-hot pain. Time seemed to stall. The pain was intense. The room sagged and swirled around her as fireworks exploded in her head.

Get up, get up, her inner mind yelled, as she could feel the warm sticky blood gushing from her head and running down her face. Then everything went black.

"Leave her. She will bleed to death. Let them find her dead. It will send a strong message," shouted Lukas as he roughly grabbed Dr. Spelman by the neck and pushed him out the door and down the stairs to their waiting van.

A petrified Dr. Spelman screamed,

"Now you've killed her, you bastards! You will never have the formula."

They explained to him, as they roughly hauled him into the alley,

"As thanks for your failure to provide the complete formula, and for the trouble you have caused us personally, in fleeing Copenhagen, not to mention The Reichmarks you were given, which incidentally we want back, the Nazi party is sending you on a relaxing train ride to a place where you can retire in peace and quiet forever. Should you just happen to remember the formula, you should let us know immediately," they said with a snarl, "because we are talking about a one-way death ticket here."

They gagged, tied and threw him in the back of the truck headfirst. Bleeding heavily, Dr. Spelman noticed the body of a woman wearing a canary yellow jacket barely concealed under a blanket. She was dead.

Klaus Barbie SS and Himmler's team would be proud of Lukas and Finn's actions on this one. The girl Anna was useless to them, now that she no longer had the formula. She would probably bleed to death anyway.

As he started the truck, Lukas looked at Finn.

"At least we got the aviation plans back from that bitch that was working with the Resistance. That's a big feather in our cap. Good thing we followed her that day. What a squeal she let out as you sliced her neck."

Finn grunted and laughed with satisfaction.

48

Anna's Paris Apartment

Anna was dying. She felt as if she were watching everything from a distance with a calm detachment. She knew she should be terrified and desperate. But all of that seemed beyond her. Anna sensed herself lifting, moving up and out of her body like floating in warm water. She felt herself roll and tumble and turned to see her body lying sprawled amidst the debris of her sitting room.

The couch cushions were slashed, their puffy guts yanked out. Both end tables were on their sides and, although one of the lamps had shattered, the other lay intact on the ground; its shade knocked away, the yellow light spilling out over millions of tiny shards of glass that surrounded her body. It was as if she were floating in space surrounded by twinkling stars, adrift forever. In the invisible current, Anna looked down at her body as it lay dying among the glass splinters.

There was a tug. Sudden, fierce. Another tug, stronger this time, and Anna was pulled down from where she had been hovering. With a dreadful searing pull, she was wrenched downward, forced back into her own body, transforming into meat and muscle and bone. As she felt herself slammed back in, every single nerve in her body painfully awoke.

Blood was everywhere. Anna screamed, but the sound was caught, burning, in her throat, arching her back as awareness of the pain detonated in her head. The aborted scream turned into a great sucking inhalation that re-inflated her lungs and popped her eyes wide. Anna clapped a hand to her head, wet, and then looked at it—bright with blood.

Awareness was back, but her memory was fragmented. She tried to grasp the how and why of her sprawled body and bloody head. The rush of blood to her head as she sat up nearly knocked her back into darkness. Why was she bleeding? A fragment of memory clicked into place, something from earlier that day. The ruble was still there, hanging from the fine gold chain under her sweater. Very slowly, as the web of nausea swept through her, the faces of Britta, Doug, Lenny and Dr. Spelman flashed in her memory. Then everything went black as Anna fell back into unconsciousness.

♦ ♦ ♦ ♦ ♦ ♦ ♦ ♦ ♦ ♦

49

The Chateau

Dumas drove, screeching to a halt in front of the apartment while cursing the French traffic. He was late, but his contact with the aviation plans never showed up and that concerned him since Margo was very reliable. Nevertheless, he parked the car and went inside Anna's apartment building taking the stairs two at a time. He would help her with her luggage and escape to the safe house today.

Anna's apartment door was wide open, and a deafening silence alerted his trained ears. Something was terribly amiss. He pulled out his weapon and proceeded cautiously, but the sight inside was one for which he was not prepared.

"Mon Dieu, what have those bastards done? Obviously, they have trailed her," he murmured, feeling her faint pulse. He gathered her up carefully in his arms and carried her down to his car. The nuns would attend to her at the chateau if he could get her there fast enough.

Arriving at the chateau at record speed, Dumas honked his horn to alert the nuns of his urgency, and then quickly carried Anna into one of the bedrooms. Dumas yelled, out of breath. "Get your medical supplies and tend to her immediately. She has suffered a severe concussion. The Germans attacked her. Her head smashed through a glass table, and she has since lost a lot of blood."

"Only time and God will determine if she can survive the severity of damage done to her body and head, Monsieur. She will need a lot of rest to heal," replied one of the nuns, modestly bowing while simultaneously trying to push Dumas out of the room so they could tend to their patient.

Dumas stood there a moment longer looking down at a still unconscious Anna. He shook his head sadly.

"Anna, Doug is coming. I promise you that he is on his way. I will get word to him immediately about what has happened."

It is my entire fault, thought Dumas sadly, as he turned and headed to the cottage. He would send a message to Alistair to contact Doug immediately.

50

The French Chateau

Some days before the Nazi bombing of Paris, Anna was recovering well at the chateau. She lived in a small room on the third floor of the chateau protected by the cloistered nuns. Anna looked around her room—a single bed with a wrought-iron head frame, a simple table with a Bible, a night lamp with a cross and her small bag containing the music box that Dumas had dropped off a few days ago. From her window, she could see a humble cottage in the distance. She noticed two nuns weeding flowerbeds.

A tear rolled down her cheek. *Living without Britta, living without Doug. I am perfectly miserable. I feel as if the wind is howling right through my lonely and broken heart,* she thought dismally. Anna spent some time writing and given the convent's vow of silence, the writing was an even more important outlet. Emotionally exhausted, she crawled back under the covers to go to sleep again. She had been sleeping for many weeks. Her body was healing well but not her spirit.

The door to her room received a gentle knock later that evening. One of the older nuns had brought her a blanket, some candles with matches, water, and a few apples with bread and cheese wrapped in a checkered napkin. The nun also delivered, finally, a coded letter from Doug.

Doug had taught her a simple code during their short but idyllic time together in Paris, foreseeing that she might need to read coded text from him. Anna quickly ripped open the letter, scribbling out the deciphered words on a piece of paper in her journal. She was to meet Doug at the Port of Barfleur on the Cotentin Peninsula, not too far from Cherbourg, where she would sail with him to England and then on to America. She was to wait for word from Dumas and go with him.

Her heart did strange little flips as she put a few things into a small bag. The nun urgently tugged at Anna's sleeve. She motioned for Anna to follow her quickly holding her index finger to her lips for absolute silence.

Suddenly, the air filled with shrill shouts, loud whistles and an insistent pounding at the door. The noise was nerve-wracking. The sound of Gestapo boots was everywhere. The Gestapo was requisitioning the chateau for its own purpose.

Anna was to quickly get into the secret tunnel and stay in hiding until it was safe to get to the port of Barfleur and until Dumas could sneak in to retrieve her. The loud banging on the front door and shouting of the German officers to open up became more insistent. It would not be long before they knocked down the front door. Quickly, the nun pulled at Anna's sleeve to follow her, while handing her the basket of provisions.

Anna followed closely as they ran into the chateau library. The heavy green damask curtains, now closed, surrounded the room in a cloak of darkness. Pulling out one of the books, the nun pushed the hidden spring. The twelve-foot tall bookshelf spun around softly, revealing a dark, cavernous opening with a few stone stairs leading down into a dark, damp tunnel. Anna was surprised, but she instinctively knew these nuns must know all the secrets of this chateau. The nun lit a candle for Anna, all the while urging her to hurry down the stairs.

The thud of the bookshelf closing behind her kicked Anna's adrenaline up a few notches. Alarmed and anxious with an overwhelming feeling of claustrophobia, she made her way along the damp passageway to the small alcove. She put down her few things and rested a moment to catch her breath. She waited a few moments to let her eyes adjust to the darkness. The walls crowded in around her.

I know I must stay here until it is safe to escape. By now, my name is probably at the top of the Gestapo most-wanted list as word has spread of my discovery. Doug had warned her that the Führer probably wanted her brought to the Kaiser Wilhelm Institute for questioning by his top scientists. This much she also knew from Dumas.

Gathering her bearings and based on her knowledge of the chateau's layout, she thought she must be right under the kitchen, which was located below ground level. There was an icebox that she could hear opening and closing above, but with the Gestapo voices just upstairs, the nuns could not get food to her. They had taken over the library as one of their offices.

She walked the length of the dark tunnel—all in all about fifty yards—holding the candle. She calculated that she might be nearing the cottage, if her sense of direction was right. Anna pushed on a small trap door at the end of the tunnel, but it did not budge. *It is possible it has not been opened in many years*, she thought. Afraid to make any noise in case the Gestapo was camped out inside the cottage too, Anna decided it might be better to wait in the tunnel a little while longer.

She crawled up in a small corner, making a bed for herself with one too-thin blanket and a few garments that served as a pillow. She sat down, drawing her knees up to her chest like a child. She hated the dark. She knew she must be careful about rationing her food because she had no idea how long she would be there. She ate a small piece of bread with cheese to quiet her growling stomach. *Thank God the dear old nun had the presence of mind to grab the basket of provisions and provide me with matches and candles.*

The darkness seemed to press in on her, and she could see her own breath. Anna shivered with the cold, and although outside it was June, the temperature in the tunnel was quite frigid. She jumped and gasped when she saw a mouse run across her blanket. The light from the candle cast eerie shadows on the wall. She was afraid to leave it burning, but equally afraid to blow out the flame. Desperation was starting to creep in, and her fitful sleep was filled with nightmares of Britta's brutal death.

◆ ◆ ◆ ◆ ◆ ◆ ◆ ◆ ◆ ◆

The blood was everywhere. Anna tried to run up the stone stairs but slipped on the blood. Her hands broke her fall, but they were covered in blood. She screamed in agony.

Anna opened her eyes and glanced slowly around as her eyes adjusted to the darkness. *Another bad dream.* Feeling disoriented and cramped from sleeping in a small, damp corner for the past few nights, she was tired and achy. Every bone in her body hurt as she felt again the injuries caused during her violent encounter with Lukas and Finn.

The last candle had gone out hours ago. *But how long ago was that? What day was it? I am losing track of time*, she thought without being able to see the passage of day and night. Searching in the darkness, she groped for matches. They were damp, but finally she got one to light what was left of the candle. *Once the last candle is gone, there will be no light to break the darkness.* Anna shuddered at the thought.

The little mouse ran across her blanket again. This time, Anna followed it's trail and saw it go out through a crack in the tunnel wall. *There is nothing I can do but wait*, she thought. *Hopefully, word will come soon. It had been the same dream every night since the day Doug had left Paris.* She took out her leather-bound journal and wrote once again to Doug, reading her letter to herself:

My dearest, my love, my soul mate, if only you were here. My heart cannot bear another moment without you. If I could have just one wish, it would be to be with you right now and for always. I cannot bear the thought of never seeing you or holding you again. I long to be in your arms, kissing your lips and holding your body close to mine. The days and hours go by so slowly without you. Never for one moment do you ever leave my thoughts. The memories of our love keep me going, although I fear my heart may burst if I do not see you again soon. I have been moved to a secret tunnel at the Chateau. The last message I received from Dumas was that I should wait for word from him and that he would arrange for my passage safely to you. I have hidden the formula inside the ruble, and continue to wait for another message from you. My dearest love, be safe. I know someday, somehow, we will be together. Nothing in the entire world can separate you from my love. Yours forever, Anna

She wished Doug or Britta were here as she held the blanket to her mouth to muffle the cough she had developed in the dampness so the sound would not be heard above the tunnel. She was feeling increasingly unwell, and her head pounded with a migraine headache.

She began to pry loose the mortar around a brick with an old knife the nun had provided with the cheese and apples. The hole was where the mouse ran in and out, near the wall by her makeshift bed. After many days of work, she could finally pull out a single brick. Encouraged by her success, Anna dug out a secure hiding place for her letters and music box in the tunnel wall. Her box now contained many other unsent letters to Doug. She placed this new letter among them.

Aware of the very real possibility that she might die in the tunnel or be captured by the Nazis, her mind churned. *If something happens to me, I must somehow hide this ruble and vial of water and yet leave an indication or clue for someone other than the Nazis to find it.* Her mind wandered as she thought of the Tetractys— the triangle with the perfect number ten. *That's it*, she thought proudly, as she proceeded to carve a symbol of the triangle on the outside of the brick to map out the location of the hiding place. Thinking that it might be too obvious, she proceeded to carve different symbols of circles and squares on some of the other bricks. It looked like a child's drawing, which is precisely what she wanted. Any person looking at it would think it was a child's doodling. Dr. Cunningham would understand it, and maybe Doug. Now she wished she had told him more.

Doug, I hope you come for me soon. I don't know how long I can bear this. Even with careful conservation of the food, she was almost out. The water was gone. As she shuffled through the letters, she glanced at the ruble that contained the complete written formula sitting at the bottom of the music box. The other ruble with the star was around her neck.

Some great universal wisdom this is, she thought sarcastically as she remembered Kathleen's words ruefully. She wondered why it mattered now—*Britta is dead, and here I am hiding under the chateau waiting for Dumas to rescue me, that is, if he can even get here.*

In the hidden compartment of the music box was the small vial with the last of the serum. Considering it carefully, she broke open the seal and drank a little of it. Resealing the vial with wax from the last candle, she placed it back in the music box and hid it in the opening she had created in the wall. All her secrets were stored there. Anna grew increasingly hungry, thirsty and delirious as her hope sank.

51

Fort Detrick
May 28th

Back in America, Doug, after meetings in Washington, had been assigned to visit a top scientist to discuss his current information on the situation in Europe. In his discussions with a scientist, Doug learned the United States sought to harbor all known germs and produce medical cures or antibodies that would protect its citizens from the threat of biochemical attack. Doug thought about Anna and her revelation to him about the molecular sequencing in the Russian sulphur spring water which had the capability to restore dysfunctional or aging cells. He did not share this. He had sworn to keep Anna's discovery secret.

I miss her, he thought, overcome by an intense longing. *I hope she is safe with Dumas at the chateau. She must have received my note by now.* He then realized what his mother and Dr. Cunningham must have felt for many years. He quickly shifted his thoughts back to the present as the scientist continued.

"Penicillin is a huge break. The development of such a drug could save millions of lives as we enter a nuclear/chemical age. We do know that Professor Karl Brandt, personal physician to Hitler, has been doing a series of medical experiments on the prisoners. Word is spreading that inmates are being purposely infected with typhus, yellow fever, smallpox, paratyphoid A and B, cholera and diphtheria. Our goal here at this facility is to study all the various strains of germs and find an antidote for many of these diseases that have plagued mankind for centuries."

"Have you made any breakthroughs? Do you think that penicillin will be available in mass quantities anytime soon? Who is making the drug and what other countries have it?" he asked.

"We certainly hope to make it available in the near future. I know Britain has made some high-grade penicillin, but in extremely small quantities. That's all we know at this point," replied the scientist, somewhat ambiguously.

Doug thanked them for the tour and departed for the next leg of the journey—The Greenbrier in West Virginia. He was meeting with The Secretary of Navy, who just happened to be teeing off at the 18th hole at the golf course. While waiting for him to complete his game, Doug used the extra time to visit the hot mineral springs advertised as 'Take the Cure at White Sulphur.'

Treatments in these facilities are modeled on those developed at the famous and ancient spas of Europe. Doug was extremely interested in this so-called "cure" now because of what Anna had confided to him about her own sulphur springs discovery. He read, "this water was highly effervescent as it flowed from the spring. Containing three to five liters of carbon dioxide per liter of mineral water, these springs contained high amounts of negative ions."

After a short wait, Doug was invited to join an exclusive, private meeting. He sat in on a debriefing of European events.

"Here is the situation in Europe. The Nazis have invaded The Netherlands, Belgium, Luxembourg and France and it looks like there is little that can stop their entry into Paris. Prime Minister Churchill has asked for our assistance and so has General Charles De Gaulle... Holland and Belgium have surrendered."

After hearing the Secretary's words, Doug's heart dropped. He needed to contact Dumas and Alistair so he could get Anna out of Paris. He was aware of most of the developments, but had held on to the hope that Paris would remain secure.

The Secretary of Navy requested that Doug join him to continue their conversation on the private railroad car back to Washington. C&O Railway, who was also part owner of the popular White Sulphur Springs resort, owned the extraordinary railroad cars. A Greenbrier chef prepared a culinary delight in the car's kitchen while the men had drinks served by Greenbrier personnel in its mahogany-paneled dining room.

A waiter had entered the train dining car and handed a telegram to the Secretary. After reading it, The Secretary of Navy handed it to Doug. His hands balled into fists as he read it. Anna had been attacked and was dying. *No, that can't be right.* Doug's distress was now visible.

The Secretary looked at him and said,

"I am sorry, son. It just came from London headquarters. We are sending you back to France to The Port of Barfleur immediately to assist the Resistance with the escape of some scientists to England. You are to escort them back to Washington. We will have an aircraft taking you to Southampton and waiting for your return with the scientists. You are to go to the Port of Barfleur and return on the boat with the scientists to England. There is a military aircraft waiting for you now. Lieutenant Anderson is already back in Paris; he should meet up with you in Barfleur. Try to contact us when you reach him, we have not heard from him."

At that moment, the waiter entered again.

"Sir," he pointed at the blinking red light in the upper right hand side of the car. Standing up, he looked at Doug,

"Excuse me son," He proceeded to open a paneled sliding door. Doug heard him pick up a phone and say, "Yes Mr.

President?" as he closed the door behind him. He could hear loud shouts but could not make out the words as the train rolled into Washington. Doug was promptly escorted off the train into a waiting car, but The Secretary was still behind closed doors in heated conversation.

52

Escape from the Chateau in Paris

In frozen horror, Anna listened as she heard scratching noises at the opposite end of the tunnel. The sound prickled her senses. Carefully, she placed the coded letter she received from Doug in her box and placed the box back inside the tunnel wall for safekeeping.

The noises above her became louder, and Anna waited, anxiously concerned that the Nazis might have discovered her hiding place. As she heard the trap door at the end of the tunnel open, her heart was thundering so loudly she could hear it in her ears. To her relief, she recognized Lenny's voice whispering her name so as not to alert any guards.

"Anna? Are you here? It's Lenny." She ran to him in joy and relief.

"Hurry, Anna, there is no time to spare. And bring the ruble."

Rushing, Anna hurried to leave the chateau grounds with Lenny. She already had the ruble on the chain around her neck. Fearful that something might happen in transit, she left her only possession—her music box with its secret treasure and her letters—in the secret hiding place she had dug in the tunnel wall.

They left the chateau through the darkness of the secret passageway and climbed out the trap door that led into the cottage. Anna's voice was scratchy from lack of use, and her eyes had trouble adjusting. All the colors were brighter than before since she was so accustomed to darkness that even the dim moonlight and starlight struck her eyes like a blow. The cottage was empty.

Crouched down under the night's blanket of darkness, they made their way off through the backside of the property to a Red Cross ambulance that Lenny had hidden off the road a few hundred feet back. Starting the engine, they headed towards the coast of France to the Port of Barfleur near Cherbourg. She was to meet Doug at the port onboard the boat. From that point, crossing the Channel to reach England should not be so difficult. Anna assumed that Dr. Cunningham and Alistair would meet them in England.

Anna—now dressed in a Red Cross nurse's uniform that was in the ambulance which Lenny stole from a nearby hospital—was hungrily devouring a baguette and Camembert cheese. In between mouthfuls, she asked,

"Lenny, tell me all the news about Doug." She also thanked him for taking care of Britta and asked awkwardly what had happened to Britta's body.

"Anna, we will talk about that later. Right now the most important thing is to get you to the port in time for the ship's departure and your rendezvous with Doug." Lenny stepped on the gas and the car lurched forward.

♦ ♦ ♦ ♦ ♦ ♦ ♦ ♦ ♦ ♦

Moments after Anna and Lenny's escape, a chauffeured car pulled into the gates of the chateau. The posted guards stopped the private vehicle. A chauffeur in a black suit was driving the sedan. Seated in the back was a seductively dressed brunette smoking a cigarette in a long black cigarette holder. She made no attempt to hide her legs with a hint of garter under the hiked-up dress as the guard shined the flashlight into the interior of the car.

"Bon soir, cheri," she said sweetly and flirtatiously. "I have been requested to see the commandant on private business."

Laughing, the guard could guess what the commandant's business with this woman of the night might be. Not wanting to intrude on his commanding officer's privacy and seeing that she was alone, he waved her through as she winked and promised to stop and see him on the way out.

Once down the driveway, Alistair turned to Dumas who was driving as the chauffeur.

"All right, Froggy. The coast is clear."

"Merci, ma belle, keep the dress on. It looks good on you. We may still be in for a Kraut surprise," joked Dumas with an underlying tone of seriousness.

Knowing there might be armed guards posted at the cottage, they passed the chateau with the lights off and pulled the car off the tree-lined driveway. Turning the engine off, they cautiously crept towards the cottage. The chateau was still, dark and very quiet.

"Bloody hell," mumbled Alistair as he tripped. He looked down—it was the body of one of the guards. His throat was cut. The dead eyes stared straight at Alistair.

Dumas reached down and touched the guard's skin to determine how long he had been dead. He concluded,

"Someone obviously got here before us but not that long ago, and it's definitely a professional job. Let's check the tunnel, but be careful. It may be booby-trapped. I'll bet they've got Anna, too."

Another dead guard's body, this one with his neck broken, lay on the other side of the cottage under the bushes. The men slowly pushed open the door, standing to the left and right side, their weapons drawn. Alistair's dress made for a bizarre contrast to the seriousness of his face and the deadliness of the weapon in his right hand. The cottage and the tunnel were empty. The kitchen cabinet that hid the Morse code transmission set, was slightly ajar, the dishes had been removed.

Dumas looked at Alistair as they both looked in the cabinet.

"Merde." Someone had broken into their transmissions.

53

Trip through Normandy

Lenny drove the ambulance over the poorly lit roads of Normandy. The journey was difficult and slow. Anna dozed in the passenger seat. Her daydream was broken with a jolt of the ambulance.

Lenny turned to Anna.

"Is that the ruble around your neck?" he asked.

"Yes," replied Anna, "it was a gift from my father. He worked as a laborer in the Russian Mint when I was a little girl. This one was discarded as defective, so he was able to give it to me."

"I didn't know you were Russian. I thought you said you grew up in Oxford. Your English is completely devoid of an accent."

"I did. And thank you for the compliment. I moved to Oxford for University when I was sixteen, so I lived in England for most of my life. My mother passed away when I was young, and my father died from injuries after an earthquake destroyed our whole village. Britta was visiting me at the time. That was when she came to live with me for good. She speaks…spoke…with even less of an accent than I do."

"Ah, yes, the beautiful Britta. I am so sorry, Anna. What a horrible night that was. I was lucky to have escaped with the help of the Embassy. There was no way to contact you and Doug. Incidentally, why don't you let me hang on to the ruble for now? Who knows what kind of trouble we could run into on the road?"

Anna gulped; she was still not feeling well. She could not talk as she struggled to hold back the tears when she thought of Britta. Instead, she started to unclasp the ruble from the gold chain around her neck and, once it was free, handed the ruble to Lenny. Anna was too busy refastening the chain around her neck to notice the odd look of satisfaction on Lenny's face.

Lenny changed the subject quickly, telling her that the boat would depart promptly at 0500. They had to hurry now so she would not miss its departure.

"This boat will not wait. We must hurry, Anna," Lenny said. He pushed down harder on the accelerator and the Red Cross ambulance jumped forward.

"Doug will be onboard waiting for you." He added glancing at her with a smile.

Anna smiled at this and sighed with relief.

It was nearly 4:45am as they approached the Port of Barfleur. Frantic refugees were jamming the road everywhere with their possessions piled up in carts. People were fighting to get onto the ship in the harbor as the word had spread among the villagers. Some had even jumped into the water and were swimming for the hull of the ship. The ship had already removed the gangplank and was moving slowly out of the harbor. Anna was among the people desperately pushing her way towards the departing ship, ignoring the hysteria surrounding her.

Dressed in a white Red Cross uniform that separated her from the gray outfits in the crowd, her platinum hair also stood out in the sea of brunette heads. Anna looked desperately for Doug, but she could not find him in the crowd. Desperation started spreading throughout her. She realized she couldn't possibly make it to the boat on time. There were just too many people blocking her way. "Lenny, help me," she shouted, but as Anna turned around, Lenny was nowhere near her.

♦ ♦ ♦ ♦ ♦ ♦ ♦ ♦ ♦ ♦

Just a few hours away, Paris had fallen to the Nazi forces.

A few minutes earlier, Doug had arrived in Barfleur at the opposite end of the hysterical mass of people. Looking through the dense crowd, he could not find Anna at first. He thought she might already be on the junket. Muscling his way through the crowd, he made it onto the boat just before the gangplank lifted and the boat began to move.

He began searching through the hundreds of people aboard looking for any sign of her. His eye caught a blonde woman. "Anna," he shouted, hopeful, but when the woman turned around, it was not Anna.

At the same time, Anna could not move an inch in the crowd. As she managed to fight her way to the edge of the dock, the ship was already on its way. She searched for Doug, but did not see him. She shouted, "Doug," but her voice was drowned out with all the noise. Everyone there wanted out of this country, out of this war. When the ship started its journey, the crowd hysteria reached an even higher pitch.

Anna wanted to be with Doug—her refuge, her love. She watched in desperation as the ship pulled away.

54

The Explosion

As the ship began moving out to sea, Doug looked back towards the port and saw a woman with platinum hair wearing a white dress. He knew it was Anna. Doug immediately pushed his way to the side of the ship, jumped off and started swimming as quickly as he could towards the port. He was far enough out that she could not see him in the water. He swam feverishly toward the dock.

In the distance, the roar of a plane sounded as the crowd looked up nervously. Anna began to fight her way back out of the horde. The ship was now at least a hundred yards offshore. Suddenly, everyone's attention was drawn to the loud sound of an engine overhead. A Nazi plane zoomed in close and bombed the ship with a single direct hit.

Lenny looked up; the plan had worked, but too late. He knew it was a Luftwaffe dive bomber, the Stuka, intentionally built with a fan like a siren under its wing, so when it dove, it made a loud shrill sound designed to inflict fear into its victims and damage their morale.

Lenny realized quickly that he needed to improvise. *Time to go to Plan B*, he thought quickly. He would have to take Anna with him.

Doug, submerged, resurfaced to replenish his lungs with air and kept his eye on Anna standing on the quay. Along with everyone else, Anna had fixed her attention on the Nazi plane. The ship sank in a massive explosion, bursting into a million pieces. Anna collapsed, not having seen Doug jump overboard; she was certain that no one could have survived.

Suddenly, the refugees that had not made it onto the ship were running everywhere, frantically seeking cover. Doug felt the heat from the flames of the exploding boat as soon as they erupted. He took heart knowing that Anna had not reached the ship. Doug muscled his way against the strong tides and tricky currents.

About forty feet from the dock now, Doug floated in the harbor, processing the disaster he had just witnessed. He was concerned about Anna's perception of the event. He noticed she was no longer standing in the spot where she had been when he last glimpsed her. He continued to swim faster to shore. Exhausted from the effort, he felt lightheaded, as if about to black out, just as he reached the dock, clinging to the wood like a lifeline.

55

Bombing of boat in Barfleur

Anna stood up, immobilized and shaking, her eyes transfixed on the column of smoke marking the spot where the ship had just been. Lenny, who had been watching the scene from a little further back, now caught up to Anna. The look of anger on his face puzzled her.

"We must go now, Anna!" Lenny urgently shouted over the noise, roughly grabbing her arm.

"I know of a safe place only a short distance from here. Let's go! That plane may be back—hurry!"

Anna looked at him in a hypnotic trance. Lenny, now thoroughly angry, roughly yanked her by the arm and pushed her back into the ambulance.

Alistair and Dumas arrived in Barfleur just moments behind Anna and Lenny. Alistair, peering from behind a wall, saw Lenny drive off in the Red Cross ambulance with Anna. Dumas, who had organized the whole escape, was horrified to see the wreckage and realized that someone had tipped off the Germans about the junket—it had been no coincidence that the German plane was flying overhead. The bombing had clearly been planned.

Witnessing Lenny's actions, he ran over to Alistair who was now huddled with another man who handed him a piece of paper.

"Froggy, this is a big problem. One of my men has just given me this intercepted message that was sent to the Germans regarding the departure time of the junket. It states that the female scientist would be onboard, and furthermore, it seems that it was sent from our cottage at the chateau. I think we know who did this."

They both rushed towards the dock. Dumas swore loudly in French, fully understanding the implications. The only code they ever used from the cottage was Basque code, and no one other than Dumas and Alistair knew that. This particular message had not been transmitted in Basque code.

56

Port of Barfleur—to Warehouse
June 15th

Lenny picked up speed in the ambulance with a shaken Anna in tow. Unscathed from the horrific scene, Anna suddenly realized that Lenny could not have known about the ruble. She had told no one but Britta and Doug. Both of them had been sworn to secrecy. Britta was dead, and Doug would never betray her. Furthermore, she remembered Doug had told her to go with no one but Dumas.

Anna tried to stay focused as she thought through what was happening. *Something was obviously very wrong. Now Doug is dead, and I was supposed to be on that ship with him. If Lenny had not arrived two minutes late, I would have been on the ship and would be dead too, and Lenny would be left with the ruble.* Willing herself to stay calm, she planned to wait for the opportunity to jump out of the ambulance. She would make her escape, but only when there were other people nearby who could help and protect her.

"Lenny, give me back the ruble," demanded Anna.

"Shut up, Anna; the ruble is now mine and worth a lot of money once I hand it over to the Germans. Too bad you didn't make the ship, now I will have to dispose of you in another way. At least your lover boy was on the boat," growled Lenny.

Anna's heart sank as she realized Lenny's scheme.

"How did you know about the ruble?" asked Anna.

249

Smugly, Lenny turned to her,

"Britta was very accommodating."

They traveled down a few side streets and then pulled in behind a warehouse—a two-story stone building, several centuries old. Most of the windows were broken, and it looked deserted. Trash and debris, accumulated from years of neglect, were scattered around the grounds. Lenny drove the ambulance around to the side of the warehouse, shut off the engine and got out, moving to the passenger door. Anna refused to move from the ambulance, holding tightly to the door handle. Lenny forcibly removed her, wrestling her into the building through the back door.

◆ ◆ ◆ ◆ ◆ ◆ ◆ ◆ ◆ ◆

Exhausted, Doug let himself rest a moment, filling his lungs with air before trying to pull himself out of the water. Gathering his strength, he managed to climb up the ladder and onto the dock, collapsing onto the wooden slats. Both Alistair and Dumas, who had rushed to the waterfront, were astonished to see him, amazed that anyone could have possibly survived such a massive explosion. As the two men hoisted his drenched body to a nearby bench, Doug thrashed violently, completely disengaged from the rescue effort.

"What the hell happened? That was a Stuka bomber!" He demanded fiercely, although still gasping for breath.

"Where is Anna? I saw her standing on the dock. That's why I jumped off the damn boat, so I could be with her."

They quickly related how Lenny had taken off with her in the ambulance. Doug's eyes were still darting about when he saw Dr. Cunningham frantically making his way towards them, visibly shaken, his face ashen.

"Douglas, thank God you are all right, son. I knew you and Anna were going to be on the boat. I arrived early to make sure my eight Jewish scientists were all safely on board. I looked everywhere for you." He turned to Dumas,

"I thought you were getting Anna from the chateau? She was supposed to be on board as well."

Dumas replied,

"We got to the chateau and Anna was gone. As we were running over to the dock we spotted Lenny pushing her into a Red Cross ambulance."

Dr. Cunningham answered,

"Obviously we have a communication breakdown somewhere along the line. We have to find Lenny, Douglas. I have a feeling he is behind all this. We must get to him and Anna as quickly as possible."

Dr. Cunningham took off his coat and the extra sweater he was wearing and handed them to his son.

"Here, put these dry clothes on."

Doug pulled them on fast, so concerned for Anna that he wanted to leave right away with no further talk. The woman he loved was in great danger. Fortune could not be so cruel.

"Bloody hell, Doug," said Alistair. "Thank God, you had the presence of mind to get off that boat. Dumas and I got here as quickly as we could. The chateau was empty, and someone broke into the transmission at the cottage. The guards were killed, so we knew this wasn't a Nazi plot." Dumas looked somberly at Doug.

"We never told you or Lenny that we were using Basque code at the chateau. There was a transmission sent from there earlier today. I got your message that you were in Barfleur and to bring Anna to you, so it had to be Lenny who went to the chateau to get Anna. He had to be the one who sent the message from the cottage, received by the Germans. No one else knew about the cottage or the boat. They sent a Stuka bomber plane out right away to destroy the refugee ship, thinking the two of you would be onboard."

Doug's mind raced as he was still trying to catch his breath. His leg was bleeding. He flinched as Dr. Cunningham tended to it quickly. "Douglas, do you still have the tracking fly I gave you?"

Doug looked at him and shook his head.

"I took it off in Brussels and gave it to Anna."

Cunningham shook his head.

"Well, never mind, at least you're alive. If she's got it on her perhaps we can get London to track her but it may be too late."

Alistair and Dumas had no idea where Lenny had taken Anna. Alistair ran down a side street and out of sight. A few minutes later, he returned with the chauffeured car they had driven from the chateau. The four men piled in. As they began to search for signs of Anna and Lenny, Dumas told Doug about all that had been happening while he had been in the US.

"We have a serious problem here. One of the transmissions leaked to the Germans gave detailed information about the junket leaving and stated that you and Anna would definitely be onboard along with the scientists. The transmission specifically indicated that the boat would be leaving at 5 a.m."

"In addition, Doug, the London office has just intercepted additional messages indicating your 'friend,' Lenny, has been masterminding behind-the-scenes espionage. We now have proof that Lenny was offered a great deal of money to provide the Germans with a 'secret', which would help them to secure confidential scientific information. And they indicated that this 'secret' was worked on by Anna and her superior, Dr. Spelman."

Doug stared at Cunningham in disbelief.

"Lenny knew I planned to be on that boat with Anna. Why would he inform the Germans we would be on the boat?

Unless his only thought was to have us killed, knowing that Anna somehow is in control of this 'secret' that she and Dr. Spelman worked on. I didn't tell him, so how did he find out about the formula?

"Damn it. *Where* could Lenny take Anna? How could I have missed the signs that he was fucking us all? That must be why my instructions told me to use Basque code always and tell no one, not even Lenny. Obviously Washington knew something." Doug ground out the words with rage.

Doug's training kicked in as his mind focused on their immediate problem. They must find Lenny and get to Anna before he could harm her. He would hash through the dynamics of the screwed-up Lenny issue later.

They quickly drove out of the port of Barfleur. A few miles outside of the village, they came across a disabled truck blocking the road. Some French farmers were repairing their broken-down vehicle.

Alistair stopped and in perfect French asked,

"Have either of you seen any kind of vehicle pass by here recently?"

"That would have been impossible since our truck has been blocking the road for the past hour. Only an ambulance with a man and a blonde nurse tried to get through, but they turned around. That was maybe twenty minutes ago. No one else," they answered cordially.

The men realized that Lenny must still be in the vicinity. They turned around, and began to drive back toward the port of Barfleur.

◆　◆　◆　◆　◆　◆　◆　◆　◆　◆

Inside the dark deserted warehouse, streams of hazy sunlight filtered in through broken panes of glass. Lenny roughly forced Anna into the main room. Old crates piled up near the entrance showed the years of rot and dirt. The middle of the room was bare except for a single folding chair. Lenny pushed Anna to sit in the chair.

When she tried to rise and run, he shoved her down again, yelling, "Now I'll have to tie you to it!" Lenny started to tie her to the chair with a ball of twine as Anna struggled against him.

"I thought you were Doug's friend! You are a traitor, Lenny!" screamed Anna.

Lenny began pacing the floor anxiously as if waiting for someone else to arrive.

A few minutes later, the back door to the warehouse opened, and Anna was stunned to see Britta enter. Startled to see her sister alive, Anna's joy turned to anger and fear when a bitter and hardened Britta produced a pistol and demanded the ruble, looking at both of them. Lenny threw her the ruble that he had taken from his pocket, not moving too far from Anna's chair. Britta missed the coin. As the ruble hit the ground, it opened and the five-star pentacle rolled to a halt right at Britta's feet. Her face turning red with anger, she picked up the ruble and began to examine it.

◆ ◆ ◆ ◆ ◆ ◆ ◆ ◆ ◆ ◆

Alistair, Doug and Dumas drove down several worn, neglected streets until they passed by a glass-shattered, deserted warehouse.

"Wait!" Doug shouted. "What's that sticking out from under the brush? See, over there!"

He pointed to a bit of white sticking out from under some hastily piled brush that only partly concealed a vehicle. Doug jumped out to inspect it, then ran back to Dumas, Dr. Cunningham and Alistair.

"They said they were driving an ambulance. They must be inside or nearby."

Alistair handed over an extra rifle.

"I'm going to kill that bastard if he hurt Anna," Doug whispered angrily. They approached the front of the warehouse silently.

Outside, Doug and Alistair crouched down, looked in through a dirty window, and saw Lenny, Britta and Anna. They also saw Britta pointing a gun at Anna, who was tied to the only chair in the desolate building.

"Damn, it's not just Lenny! Britta is alive! What the hell is going on? She must have faked her own death with Lenny's help while Anna and I were having dinner that night. The pieces are all starting to come together," Doug exclaimed.

"Britta must have told Lenny about Anna's discovery that night after the jazz club. That's why she would not even look at me when she came home late and cut herself on the glass vase. She asked Anna how much the discovery was worth. I attributed it to too much champagne. She is involved in all of this in a very bad way."

"Considering she is holding a pistol on her sister, I would agree. Remember how friendly she was with the Russian owner of that jazz club on the night of her birthday? By the way, faking your own death by using the blood of an animal is an old trick," Alistair added, keeping his voice low.

Strategizing, Doug quickly took control.

"Alistair, you and Cunningham go around to the back of the warehouse. Count to two, then come crashing in through the rear door. Dumas and I will come in through the front. Let's try to keep the gunplay to a minimum—aim to maim, not to kill. We want them alive, or we'll never get the answers we need. Our first priority is to get Anna out."

♦ ♦ ♦ ♦ ♦ ♦ ♦ ♦ ♦ ♦

57

The Warehouse

Lenny turned to a calculating Britta, only to see that she had now turned the pistol on him. Gone were all traces of the sick and vulnerable girl. In her place, stood a vindictive woman, with pure hatred in her eyes. Lenny now realized he had met his match; Britta had been playing him also. She picked up the ruble, but it was empty; the five-star pentacle had rolled onto the filthy floor and had stopped right at her feet. Lenny never had time to examine the ruble before handing it over to her.

She picked up the ruble and began to examine the coin while keeping the pistol pointed at both Lenny and Anna. To her horror, Britta quickly realized that Anna had given them the wrong ruble. This one did not contain the microfilm in it that she needed to make her deal with the Russians. Viktor would be very angry. She turned on Anna and backhanded her brutally. Anna's head snapped sideways from the impact, and her lip began to bleed, but she couldn't raise her hand to brush away the blood.

"You bitch! Where is the microfilm and the serum? You were always the smart one, so beautiful—Anna, always in the limelight," Britta sneered. "If only you knew how much I've always hated you. Now at last, it's my turn.

"Give me the microfilm. I can start a completely new life with the money the Russians will give me for that formula. It is after all from the Russian spring, and it rightfully should be theirs. This deal will make me so powerful that I will never be the ignored invalid again. And you can't fool me. This is the wrong coin. Our father gave you two rubles. Where is the microfilm? Where have you hidden that second ruble?" Britta began searching through Anna's clothing, looking for a concealed pocket where she might have hidden it.

Anna, her anger rising at the shock of Britta's sudden reappearance, replied furiously,

"You told Lenny about the serum, didn't you? I don't know where it is. I must have lost it in the ocean. Britta, what has happened to you? I don't understand any of this. I worked on this formula to try to help you and now you would turn on me—for what? Money? Don't be so foolish, Britta."

Britta looked at Anna, her eyes snapping hatred. "Shut up!"

This was not the sister Anna remembered. Perhaps that girl was only an illusion. *Certainly this unrecognizable harridan must have been concealing her true character for a long time. Could it be possible that the formula had changed her?* Anna's scientific mind churned, desperately trying to find a reason for Britta's crazy behavior.

Britta ignored her and looked at Lenny, her screaming now bordering on hysteria. "You ass! You were supposed to make sure she had the microfilm! Where is my half of the money from the German deal, Lenny? You never intended to share it, did you?"

"Britta, they wanted the formula first. We were supposed to meet them after the boat explosion," Lenny started to explain when suddenly Doug and Dumas burst through the front door, followed by Alistair and Dr. Cunningham crashing through the back door. Lenny pushed Anna aside, and she fell to the floor, still bound to the chair. Britta turned to confront Doug and Dumas and fired a round of bullets in their direction. Both men took cover behind a crate.

Meanwhile, Lenny aimed his pistol and fired a shot at Alistair who ducked quickly behind another crate. Lenny's shot drew Britta's attention, and she turned her pistol back to Lenny. But he was quicker, firing a single shot which hit Britta in the smack in her forehead. She dropped to the floor, clasping her free hand to her head where the bullet had entered. Without a moment's hesitation Alistair lined up his shot directly at Lenny's chest, fired two shots and blew him off his feet, killing him instantly.

Britta, in one final effort, lifted her bleeding head, pointed the gun at Doug and squeezed the trigger. Dr. Cunningham, with one rapid-fire move, pushed Doug aside and took the bullet for his son—it hit him directly in the chest. Britta had killed the one man who had treated her as if she were his daughter.

Grabbing his chest, now red from spurting blood, Dr. Cunningham groaned, his breathing labored,

"Why, Britta?"

Doug rushed over to Anna to untie her from the chair and helped her up from the floor. Brushing debris from her hair, he kissed her pale, still-stunned face. Anna swayed slightly in his arms. Doug, whom she thought was dead, was alive. Britta had actually been alive all this time and now was dead again, a stranger to them all. Anna looked over at her sister's body, and tears began to flow freely. Britta had died before she had given up any answers, and so much worse, had also caused the deaths of Lenny and Dr. Cunningham!

Anna held on to Doug tightly as she kissed him, making sure he was finally real, not just a dream. They quickly ran over to Dr. Cunningham and tried to stop the bleeding. Anna reached for a piece of broken glass on the floor. Doug looked at her quickly with concern as he pressed down on Dr. Cunningham's chest to try to stop the blood flow.

"Doug, I drank some of that serum while I was hiding in the tunnel. If it is still in my system maybe…"

"Anna don't!" but she had already cut her finger and was squeezing blood from it into Dr. Cunningham's chest. Doug looked at her somberly

"It's too late Anna, the bullet went through his aorta."

With a trembling hand, Dr. Cunningham reached into his pocket and handed Doug a card with the letter "C" embossed on it and a number.

"Douglas, the Tetractys," he managed to whisper as he grasped Doug's hand, and with one last breath and a transcendent look on his face, Dr. Cunningham stared up to the sky that he could barely see through the cracked windows, sighed once and was gone.

Anna heard him, immediately realizing that Dr. Cunningham and his mother were both part of the Pythagorean sect. She was now sure that her own mother had tried to pass this on to her on her deathbed, along with the necklace and the notebook.

Doug was oblivious to the tear slipping down his face.

"Anna, he once told me that his sole consolation in a lonely life was that he would join my mother in heaven when he died. I hope his wish comes true."

Anna hugged Doug, feeling his pain and loss in addition to her confusion over Britta's death yet again. Anna slowly walked over to Britta's bloodied body on the floor. She picked up the pentacle star and kneeled down to hold Britta in her arms, closing her sister's eyes. She looked at her with an overwhelming sadness, still not understanding the change in her personality.

None of this would have happened if I hadn't discovered the formula, she thought. She picked up the two halves of the ruble and along with the Pentacle Star, put them in her pocket.

Dumas, watching the scene, called out to her.

"Anna, I will make all the arrangements for the bodies to be sent to England. Hurry up, you and Doug must leave immediately."

Anna kissed her sister one last time and then turned to leave with tears still slipping down her face. Doug, Alistair and Anna had to depart for Marseilles. They would take the ambulance. It was too dangerous to attempt another boat crossing.

Before leaving to rejoin his Resistance Group, Dumas gave Doug petrol for the car and instructions for the safest way south toward Marseilles. He then explained that he followed Lenny on their first night in Paris to a strip club while Doug was asleep at the hotel. So he had purposely taken them to the chateau to show them the communications setup.

Dumas added,

"Although we had no previous concrete evidence, Lenny was high on the list of suspects. He fit the psychological profile we were looking for."

Dumas' intelligence-gathering forces had learned that Lenny had started this habit of frequenting strip clubs as a teenager when his family lost their fortune and his mother turned to stripping at night for the big cash tips. Lenny had been humiliated and embarrassed by her actions.

"Becoming known as the Stripper Ripper was his revenge on his mother, and in his twisted mind, he was saving other women from a bad life." Dumas explained, "Lenny knew of an easy solution to help Britta fake her death by using the blood of animals. This scheme was supposed to have allowed her the chance for a new identity and the ability to start a new life with her Russian lover."

The record of slayings by the Stripper Ripper added up to twelve murders. Britta had been next on his list of victims. But he first needed to get rid of Anna and Doug who knew about the formula, before he killed her. Without Lenny realizing he was pitted against a similarly twisted mind, Britta had always remained one step ahead of him in the planning. She had set herself up to split the money from Lenny's sale of the microfilm to the Germans, while simultaneously arranging to sell it to the Russians through her lover, the Russian Club owner, Viktor. Britta knew the Germans would dispose of Lenny once they realized they had been double-crossed, eliminating the problem for her.

Dumas mentioned that he had purposely left out the Basque code information on their first tour of the chateau, assuming that someone would eventually try to transmit from there. The penicillin had been Dr. Cunningham's negotiation to get the eight Jewish scientists out of the work camps and eventually to the United States, approved confidentially by Donovan and FDR.

Dr. Spelman had received a large sum of money from the Germans, but by the time they realized they didn't have the whole formula, he had already transferred the money out of the country.

Dumas elaborated,

"Lukas and Finn had caught up with him at Anna's apartment in Paris and sent him on a train to his death at a concentration camp. They never found any trace of the money since the bank he had forwarded it from had since been taken over. The banker that did the transaction had been shot and killed."

Alistair joined in,

"That's when we moved all the gold. Bumping into you both was pure coincidence. Britta, it seems, had cultivated the skill of stripping while in Oxford. The club in Paris was owned by the Russian who also owned the strip club in Copenhagen. She invited Lenny that night of her birthday to go with her to the strip club after you had left."

Alistair said, "The reason I never went back in after your fight with Lukas and Finn to join you for a drink is because we knew the club owner was actively working as a Russian operative. I suspected he had recruited Britta or both of them. I waited and followed Lenny and Britta to the strip club he owned down the street. We didn't know about Anna's research with the formula at that time although we knew they were spying on the Niels Bohr Institute because of the break-throughs in technology."

Anna interrupted.

"How do you know what they said or did in there if you didn't go in after them?" she asked. "Britta must have confided my molecular discovery with Lenny that night."

"Dr. Cunningham had been working with us and with the United States. After he retired from his medical practice, he was being primed to take the place of Admiral Sir Hugh 'Quad' Sinclair, code name 'C,' head of the MI6. In his negotiations with Colonel Donovan while he was in London, Cunningham requested that Doug be assigned for this mission. It was his hope to work with his son and to protect him. It was his way of making up for all those lost years."

Alistair continued.

"Then Sinclair became ill and Cunningham started using the code name 'C.' He arranged for Doug to be picked specifically for this mission, but there were doubts all along about Lenny's loyalty. Therefore, if you were both sent over together, we could isolate Lenny and test him with decoy communications. I'm sorry we couldn't share this with you, Doug. I could only alert you about the intercepted message."

"Cunningham was a genius with inventions and developed a special tiny device that looks like a fly on the wall. It could track and act as a listening bug, literally, so we could hear him hitting the strokes for the key transmission at the cottage. Dumas helped plant it in the Paris strip club. The German was one of our operatives, knowing that Lenny would go to meet with him to try to strike a deal."

Dumas added,

"We learned Lenny was making a deal with the Germans. He figured out that Anna would be hiding at the chateau. It was also the perfect opportunity for him to use our communication setup to notify the Germans about the boat's departure." He walked over to Lenny's body and went through his pockets.

Dumas walked back over to them. "By the way, I found this piece of paper in Lenny's pocket."

As he handed the paper to Doug, who turned it over in his hand.

"This looks like part of a biology notebook. Anna?"

Anna took the scrap of paper, looked at it with immediate recognition.

"Doug, this is a piece of my last page that I burned in my fireplace at home. I think it must be the part that slipped between the cushions. I went back for it, but Britta must have taken it."

Dumas looked at her.

"She did more than just take it, ma chère. If you turn it over, you will see a Russian name on it. It is the man who owned the nightclub, apparently your sister's lover. There is also a telephone number on it belonging to your friend Margo."

Anna looked at the scrap again.

"That must have been the paper that Margo wrote on and handed to Britta when I was in the kitchen."

Alistair nodded,

"Britta had worked out a deal to sell the Russians the formula after she got the money from Lenny's sale of your work to the Germans. Spelman ruined his chances by telling the Germans you lost the final bit. With O'Grady's help, we have the Russian in custody now."

Dumas looked at Anna compassionately.

"I hope someday you will be successful in your research, Anna. We need people like you who will work for the good of mankind, rather than our destruction." Dumas handed them a can of petrol along with directions to Marseilles and hugged them both goodbye.

Alistair looked at them and said,

"Cigarette?" as he lit up another Dunhill cigarette.

58

The Trip to Freedom

There was no more time to explain or to talk with Dumas—Doug, Alistair and Anna immediately jumped in the ambulance and started their journey south. As they drove, Alistair explained to Anna that Lenny had made a deal involving large sums of money from the Nazis for the formula, relying on Britta to get it for him. Unbeknownst to him, Britta had made her own deal with the Russian club owner in Copenhagen to sell the formula to the Soviets.

Anna slowly absorbed and processed this information. She now saw how Britta had been fooling them all. She also realized that Britta's aloofness at times was in reality the inability of a psychopath to feel any emotion other than anger. *What a horrible twist of fate that Doug should lose his father just when he had found him,* thought Anna.

Doug felt angry and betrayed about losing the father he didn't know he had and discovering that his friend was actually a traitor to his country and a murderer, not to mention that Anna's sister was a psychopath.

"It doesn't get more twisted than this, Anna," Doug remarked.

Anna felt a strange sense of loss and tried to comprehend how Britta could have turned on her when she had loved her so much. A fleeting and disturbing thought crossed her mind as she wondered if the serum had the capability to change her sister to a psychotic personality. *I guess I will never* know, she thought.

Anger took over when she thought of how Dr. Cunningham gave them so much and Britta had taken everyone and everything for granted.

The sun was setting as they reached the outskirts of Marseilles. They easily boarded the British ship for Gibraltar and were safely launched out to sea as Alistair waved goodbye. A plane in the distance approached slowly, but it veered off in another direction, and everyone breathed a sigh of relief. Off the coast of Gibraltar, a US Navy ship was waiting to take them back to Norfolk, Virginia.

◆ ◆ ◆ ◆ ◆ ◆ ◆ ◆ ◆ ◆

Doug and Anna stood on the deck of the ship, as Doug spoke with one of the officers. Anna reached instinctively for her necklace. She knew the ruble with the microfilm and serum were safely hidden below the chateau. She might never see the ruble or those letters again, but she was safe, free and most importantly, with the love of her life.

A sailor looked out of one of the cabin doors. He saw the sacred pentacle representing the feminine energy of the goddess hanging from Anna's neck. It matched the tattoo on his arm. The symbol was the Star of Life, which had been the symbol of divine illumination. It was the secret sign of Pythagorean followers "so that they may know each other." It was the widespread secret symbol used since ancient times, protecting those who have it. It was not important that she know about him; for now she was safe.

Anna felt the wrinkled edge of the envelope from Dr. Spelman in her pocket but decided that given all they had gone through it was not important, at least not now. Someday, perhaps, she would open it.

Having Doug by her side made Anna smile. He winked at her as she gazed up at him. In a magical moment, he could no longer resist the impulse to kiss her. The Louis Armstrong song, "A Kiss to Build a Dream On," was playing on a radio in one of the ship's rooms, and they held each other, swaying a bit to the music. Loud applause broke out as they looked up to see the entire crew of the ship clapping and whistling.

♦ ♦ ♦ ♦ ♦ ♦ ♦ ♦ ♦ ♦

Yet, still hidden within the walls of the chateau—inside a secret passageway—was the answer to a mystery that could change the world forever. A cloistered nun swept a dusty library floor while looking out the window, longing for a day when the Germans didn't own the streets of France, not knowing that beneath her, was the passageway where Anna's Secret Legacy would remain hidden. For now.

The End

♦ ♦ ♦ ♦ ♦ ♦ ♦ ♦ ♦ ♦

SEQUEL
Mackenzie's Secret

September 1969
Le Bourget Airport—Paris

The striking young man in highly decorated military dress descended from the aircraft with his duffle bag slung over his shoulder. He saluted the General and took the large manila envelope that was handed to him. After being dismissed, he strode quickly into the airport and went directly to the men's room. Entering the stall, he promptly removed his uniform and put on the clothing he pulled out of the duffle bag. He stuffed his uniform into the bag and, wearing a priest's collar, quickly exited the airport into a waiting car.

"Where to, mon Père?" asked the driver, as he put the duffle bag in the trunk.

"To the Chateau," replied Father Sean, squinting his deep blue eyes against the glare of the sun as he reached for his sunglasses and settled into the back seat. It was only a thirty-minute ride, and, even though he knew the letter by heart, he took it out of his pocket and began to read it again. He closed his eyes briefly, listening to the car radio playing Bob Dylan's "Masters of War."

The driver easily shifted gears and maneuvered the car at racing speed toward the chateau. Twirling his grey mustache, he pulled his chauffeur hat lower over his eyes, as he glanced at Sean from the rear view mirror.

◆ ◆ ◆ ◆ ◆ ◆ ◆ ◆ ◆ ◆